LIZARD

LIZARD

Dennis Covington

Delacorte Press

Published by
Delacorte Press
Bantam Doubleday Dell Publishing Group, Inc.
666 Fifth Avenue
New York, New York 10103

Library of Congress Cataloging in Publication Data

Covington, Dennis.
Lizard / Dennis Covington.
p.   cm.
Summary: Sent by his guardian to live at a Louisiana school for
retarded boys, Lizard, a bright, deformed youngster, escapes with
the help of a visiting actor who gives him a role in his repertory
company's production of *The Tempest*.
ISBN 0-385-30307-6
[1. Physically handicapped—Fiction. 2. Theater—Fiction.
3. Louisiana—Fiction.] I. Title.
PZ7.C83449Li 1991
[Fic]—dc20   90-49789 CIP AC

Manufactured in the United States of America
June 1991
10 9 8 7 6 5 4 3 2 1
BVG

for Vicki, Ashley, and Laura

The author wishes to thank Susan Barron, who encouraged him to write this book; Vicki Covington, who gave him the faith to continue; and the Alabama State Council on the Arts, who provided him the means. Special thanks also to Mary Cash, Randy Marsh, Wayne Jones of the Leesville State School, and a boy named Lovado.

. . . when I waked,
I cried to dream again.
—CALIBAN

PROLOGUE

MY DADDY was a Cajun out of no place in particular around Bayou Teche. I asked one time to see where he grew up, but Miss Cooley said the location could only be predicted, since the water rose and fell in that part of the parish. I know what it must have been like, though. On dirt roads along the bayou I have seen those houses with broken-down porches and screen doors kicked in, flatboats overturned in the yard, and I can imagine my daddy out back on Saturday evenings, playing the accordion under the live oak tree, while the grown-ups drank beer and danced, the air sang with mosquitoes, and the nighttime came down slow on top of them all.

It was Miss Cooley that told me how my daddy died. She didn't say much, only that it was in 1963, when Hurricane Bertha, the one that appeared to be heading west toward Galveston, took a nasty turn and caught the oil rigs south of Holly Beach. I have seen all that scrap metal on the beach before, and I have asked if it was off the rigs. Miss Cooley replied, no, it was just the result of "poor people's ignorance"—old cars and washing machines and other mechanical things they had bought fourthhand in Lake Charles and never gotten to work.

Sure, I've questioned the truth about the way my daddy died. I have heard too many other boys at the Leesville State School tell the same story about their fathers. I even looked up Hurricane Bertha in a Collier's *Yearbook* of 1963, and I believe the book when it says that only three people died on account of the storm. But I also believe that my daddy just could have been one of those three. The other boys, or anyway all but two of them, have been misled along the way.

My name is Lucius Sims. You'll find out soon enough I'm smarter than I look. Nobody ever proved that I was retarded, like the rest of the boys, but if you was to see me, I'm afraid you wouldn't like me much. It's because of the way I look that Miss Cooley sent me to the state school. She was marrying somebody from upstate. I don't hold it against her. She'd waited a long time to get married. Twice before she had accepted engagement rings, but the men had skipped town without getting them back. Miss Cooley chalked up these little disasters as "poor people's ignorance," because, in fact, there was nobody poorer than Miss Cooley herself.

She was so thin that people sometimes mistook her for one of the neighborhood girls. She wore yellow bath slippers that she could hardly keep on her feet, and she carried a straw purse with a pink flamingo painted on top. She had a row of freckles across the top of her nose and a mole the size of a thumbtack stuck at her hairline. I remember now that the flamingo on her purse was chipped where it had hit the radiator. One of Miss

Cooley's front teeth was chipped too. The edge of it glistened at night when she laughed.

We lived above the L&N Café in De Ridder, Louisiana. We had a daybed in our room, a cage for whatever I could get Miss Cooley to let me keep, and a window box with sweet-potato vines in it. When Miss Cooley worked at the café downstairs, I'd stay all day in the room, watching my blue-tailed skink eat wasp larvae.

Those times when business downstairs was slow, Miss Cooley would come home early. She'd try to read a magazine but get stuck on words and throw the book down, saying, "Oh, who cares what some movie star said!" And on Fridays she'd make lemonade for one of her boyfriends, who would sit in the white chair near the window, jiggling his change and laughing when nothing at all was funny. When the boyfriend had left, Miss Cooley would grab me by the shoulders and say, "What am I going to do with you underfoot all the time?"

When I look in the mirror, I must not see it the way everybody else does. It's just Lucius Sims staring back at me—my shoulders and neck, my face, my eyes. Sure, my eyes are more on the sides of my head than most people's, but they're a real nice color, kind of like seawater. I don't even have to wear glasses. People just think I can't see good because my eyes look in different directions. They also think, because my nose lays down on its side, that I can't breathe right. One time Miss Cooley and I were on a train that hit a stalled truck. When the conductor saw me, he yelled for an ambulance, though I wasn't hurt. "Breathe through your mouth!" he kept telling me.

People think it's my face and the way my shoulders are humped and the way I still limp a little (even though Miss Cooley has said she thought the one leg was catching up with the other)—they think it's all this that makes me different from everybody else. But I don't buy that. I mean, I know I am different. And it worries me some. I think about it at night when beds creak and in the morning when garbage men rattle cans in the alley. But I also know that the way I look is not the reason I am different. It is only the outward sign.

1

FROM THE outside it looked like an ordinary school—square and tall and streaked white where pigeons had been. Most of the windows on the top floor were open, a few with geraniums in them. But the ground-floor windows were shut tight. Off to the side stood a playground with two seesaws and a rusted swing set. The thing that made the school different was the chain-link fence and barbed wire that separated the playground from the street.

A woman in white stood waiting for me in the shadow of a crape myrtle tree. The wind had whipped her frizzy blond hair so far to one side that it looked like she might tump over. She squinted at the piece of paper Miss Cooley had pinned to my shirt and said my name under her breath.

"That bus is never on time," she added aloud as she took my overnight bag. "I'm Nurse Barmore. Just do like I say and we'll get along fine."

Miss Cooley had said almost the exact same thing that morning as she tried to pin the note to my shirt without sticking me. We had been standing under the awning at the De Ridder bus stop, which was really just a corner of the Texaco station next to Smithers's barber shop. The bus door was open, and the driver was gunning the engine every now and then.

"Just do what they tell you and you'll get along fine," Miss Cooley had said. "I'll let you know when Alton and me get settled. Maybe this won't last a real long time."

I looked at her with first one eye and then the other.

"Now, don't start that," she said to me, though I hadn't started anything. "He's set in his ways, but maybe sometime you can come visit, okay?"

She was talking about her fiancé from upstate, Alton Broussard, a man I had never seen or heard except through the exhaust fan above the side door of the L&N Café. When the fan wasn't running, I had found I could eavesdrop on conversations from the lowest branch of a nearby sweet gum tree.

Miss Cooley had met Broussard at the café. She said he was a salesman for an oil-pipe company, a big tipper, and she had never brought him upstairs to meet me.

"There," Miss Cooley said when she got the note pinned. Then she pushed the hair off my forehead. She was wearing her bath slippers and Sunday School dress, an off-white shift that was missing a sash.

"I ain't got all day, lady," the bus driver said.

She stared up at him with a fierceness I hadn't seen since her last boyfriend, a loudmouthed sergeant from Fort Polk, had chunked a rock through her window screen. It was the sergeant's overnight bag I was carrying my stuff in.

"You know he's never been on a bus alone, don't you?" Her hand was raised to shield her eyes. It was only May, but nearly ninety degrees.

"Yes, ma'am, you have already told me that," the driver said. He wore clip-on sunglasses and a bolo tie.

"It's the Leesville State School for Retarded Boys," she added.

"I have stopped there many a time," the driver said.

She started to say something more to the driver but must have thought better of it. "Well, go on, now," she said to me. And even after I was halfway up the steps of the bus, she repeated, "Go on, now" barely loud enough for me to hear.

"Watch the curb," Nurse Barmore said. I stepped onto the sidewalk and swiveled my head to get a look around. On the other side of the chain-link fence stood a fat boy in a ripped T-shirt. He was listening to a transistor radio, his eyes as motionless as dead leaves in a pond.

"What're you looking at?" he asked.

"Nothing."

He scowled and spit into the dirt. "I'm the one that ought to be looking," he said.

"Get back with the others, Walrus," Nurse Barmore said. "I mean this instant."

Then she took my hand and hurried me through the gate and into the dark hallway of the Leesville State School. A bell had just rung, and boys were streaming down the stairs at either end of the hall, pushing and shouting at each other as they came. Nearby there was a scuffling of feet. Somebody had tried to trip Nurse Barmore and when she swung an elbow at him, he backed against the wall. I couldn't see his face, but the light from a high window fell across his right arm, which was shriveled all the way to his shoulder.

"I'll bite your tit off, you old bag!" he said.

"And I'll see you in the quiet room," she answered.

"Both tits!" he screeched as he raced away.

Now I could make out other boys sidling along the wall to the right of us and limping backward into the dark. There was a fight going on in a side hall that ended with the boys on the floor in a tangle, like an octopus with its legs waving at me.

"Please," I said, fighting to loosen Nurse Barmore's grip. But she jerked me ahead.

"This ain't anything," she said.

At the far end of the hall I saw something that made me struggle even harder. Two faces, as white as the stone angels on top of a cemetery gate, were gliding in and out of the shadows. I buried my head in Nurse Barmore's stomach, but I saw their eyes as they floated past us—tiny and red, like blind mice.

"You've never seen albinos?" she said.

She led me out the door at the end of the hall and into the sunlight again. I could see what looked like a gymnasium and a parking lot with two basketball hoops, no nets. At the edge of the parking lot was an oak tree and an incinerator. Behind them stretched a field of uncut weeds that ended at the fence.

We walked under an aluminum shed and into a cinderblock building. My hands were sweating by the time she got me to my bunk in a long room with windows. There were two sleeping bays, she said, one for the boys under ten, and this one for the older boys like me. Each bay had a double row of bunks, maybe thirty altogether. Mine was in the dead center of the double rows. "You're going to like it here, Lucius," Nurse Barmore said. She dumped the stuff from my overnight bag into a footlocker and folded a towel across the bedstead. "We're a big family."

At supper I overheard Walrus say, "His head looks like a turd." The boy with the shriveled arm laughed. So did the midgets and the boy without any hands and the bucktoothed albinos, who must have been cousins or brothers.

"He smells like one too," said the boy with the shriveled arm, and the black boy they called Ricardo laughed so hard, his false teeth fell into the mashed potatoes.

Dessert was peach cobbler, but I couldn't eat any.

Afterwards, a red-faced man in a green work shirt got everybody's attention by banging an ax handle on the edge of the piano.

"Listen up, boys," he said. "There won't be any bingo tonight. Nobody to call the numbers." The boys groaned. "But canteen'll set up as usual right afterwards. The limit is one candy bar or a pack of gum, not both. And there ain't no Snickers this week." Another groan. "Only you boys that are fourteen and older and that helped set up the dining room tonight are eligible for cigarettes."

"Shit," said the boy with the shriveled arm.

"What do you care, crip?" said Ricardo. "You don't smoke." He was drumming on the edge of the table with his knife and fork.

"I'm thinking about starting," the boy replied with some heat.

"Get ahold of yourselves, boys," the man said, and he banged the ax handle slowly against the piano again.

"There's only one week left of your regular classes." Someone let out a whoop. "But small-engine repair and woodworking will continue during the summer, and I'll be here every day as usual to make sure you don't get into trouble with all the free time that's on your hands."

"When we going swimming, Mr. Tinker?" the boy with the shriveled arm yelled.

"If you have a question, raise your hand," the man said. "But to answer your question, yes, we are going swimming some at Alligator Lake this summer, and there'll be Tarzan movies on Friday nights, and your bingo of course, and maybe some special surprises."

"Like what?" the boy without any hands shouted.

"I said to raise your hand if you have a question," Mr. Tinker replied with some heat. He reddened when he saw his mistake, and the other boys nearly went into fits.

He pounded the ax handle. "That's all I've got to say for tonight. I'll be posting your work orders for the week on the door of your bay, and those of you who can read help the others out."

The dining hall erupted in the sound of voices and the scrape of chairs.

"I wonder if old Turd Head can read," the boy with the shriveled arm said above the din.

Walrus was adjusting his radio. "I wonder if he can swim," he replied without a smile.

The social worker that interviewed me chain-smoked Salem Lights and spent most of the hour talking about her son, who was a junior in high school and giving her all kinds of trouble. She didn't like his friends or his clothes or the way he wore his hair. "He treats me like hired help," she said, and then she broke down crying and said her problems were all due to the fact that her father used to whip her with a belt when she was growing up. When I asked what she did to get whipped with a belt, she gave me a funny look.

Nurse Barmore did my physical exam. She was swift and for the most part gentle, despite the way she talked. When she was weighing me and getting my height, she kept telling me to stand up straight, which I have never been too good at. "Well, at least you don't have a weight problem," she said. Then she told me to take off my shorts, bend over, and hold on to the table, and that was the part that hurt.

The next day the barber cut my hair too short, and a psychologist I'd never see again put me through his stuff. The other boys were in class while all this was going on. I'd see them in the hall on my way from one place to another, and they'd point at me and make farting sounds. I never said a word to any of them. As far as they knew, I was deaf and dumb. It made it easier for me to get by at night, when they were loud and mean and looking for somebody to get even with.

Soon I had a routine. Every morning I limped to breakfast, the last in line. Then I'd go to my work assignment—my favorite was waxing the floors in the main building, where it was cool and dark, and the supervisor, a grown man who really was retarded, never said anything unkind. Most afternoons I'd watch the other boys try to take apart lawn-mower engines in Mr. Tinker's class. At night I'd skip bingo and go to bed early. My bunk was between Ricardo's and the boy without any hands. I slept with the cover over my head. But even then I knew this was a lonely way to live. By June I had gotten up enough nerve to walk outside toward the back fence, past Mr. Tinker and a group of boys cutting weeds with swing blades. Their backs were as glossy in the sun as caramels. I thought they hadn't noticed me, but when Mr. Tinker went inside the gym for a minute, one of the boys took off running and tackled me in the tall grass. It was the boy with the shriveled arm.

"I'm mean as a skunk," he said, scrambling on top of me. "I bit the barber."

"Get off!" I said, forgetting I wasn't supposed to be able to talk.

"I drink whiskey before breakfast, and anybody who says I don't, I give 'em this." He stuck his fist in my face.

I wrestled with him. He tried to bite my arm, but I finally shoved him off of me. "I know who stole Mr. Tinker's glasses," he said, "but I don't want to tell you!" Then he scrambled to his feet and ran away, his right arm waggling.

Somebody far off yelled, "Turd Head!" in my direction, but I got up and kept walking toward the fence. The cold wire felt good between my fingers. A ditch, red as a popped blister, made a turn on the other side of the fence. There wasn't any water in it, just Zero wrappers and cigarette butts. A mockingbird swooped down and started snooping under the wrappers.

Suddenly I was jerked from behind. It was that boy again. "I'm telling you I bit that barber. He was a grown man, but you should have seen him cry. Ask anybody around here who Mike is. They'll tell you."

"Mike who?" I asked.

"Gimme a weed." He snatched the Salem I had gotten for putting a second coat of wax on the first-floor hallway, and tore the filter off. He took two deep puffs, throwing his head back and squinting. Then he tossed the cigarette over the fence. "Shit, that ain't so good," he said. "What are you looking at, anyway?"

"I thought there was a creek back here." Past Mike's shoulder I could see the other boys playing chase in the knee-high grass. "That boy with the radio," I said. "He's mean, ain't he?"

Mike turned on me in a fury. "Walrus is my brother, so be careful what you say. We used to live on a boat," he said as he twisted my arm behind my back.

"Okay, I believe you," I said.

Mike let go of me and fell back against the fence, tugging at the grass while he laughed high like a horse. "You should have seen that boat," he finally said. Then a look of panic crossed his face.

"What's wrong?"

"There's a cloud coming." And sure enough, the sunlight began to fade. The air turned cold and still. I looked through the fence at the ditch and the mockingbird fishing under a Coke cup. The sun came back after a minute, but Mike had vanished.

After some hunting I found a place where I could sit and not be seen by the other boys. Behind the gymnasium, near the back fence, was a water oak with a curved place near its bottom. The bark was cold and rough, filled with holes where insects lived. I'd pretend I was leaning into a comfortable old chair, watching the field beyond the fence, the weeds and dragonflies. I'd imagine I was in the backyard of a white house with flowers along the porch and a creek crossed by a bridge, a house like I had seen in Newllano from the bus window on the way to the school.

I didn't even tell Mike where I hid, although he had

begun to act like he wanted to be friends. He sneaked orange juice from the kitchen to share with me in the broom closet after lights out, then told me how his arm had gotten run over by a motorcycle policeman. "It killed the cop," he confided, rolling up his sleeve to show me what he said were tread marks across the twisted skin near his shoulder. Mike knew how to get extra food from the cook, who had a good heart and four gold teeth. While the other boys slept, he filled me in on how to slip by in small-engine repair without getting on Mr. Tinker's bad side. "Play dumb," he said. And he was the first to show me the quiet room. It wasn't a room at all, but an empty shower stall with bars, where you spent the weekend if you pitched a fit. Mike said he'd been locked up there plenty of times. Then his voice got weird and he said that once Nurse Barmore had hit him with the butt of a submachine gun, which is why he had a tooth missing and a scar down the back of his head. He told me not to cross Nurse Barmore. He also warned me to stay away from the albinos, because they could see through walls.

On Saturdays we sat together on the blue school bus that took us to Alligator Lake, where there was a long wooden pier and a place roped off for swimming. Mike always did a sidestroke with his good arm. He said he was practicing for the day when he would swim all the way across the lake. In the sunlight, without my shirt on, I knew that I looked skinny and weak. In the water, though, I was quick and strong. I especially liked to swim underwater because nobody could find me there. It felt good to go deep, where the slick plants grazed my face, and the mud where I touched bottom was like nothing I had ever touched before, so cool and soft I wouldn't have minded getting lost in it. The only bad part was having to come up for air.

When I did come up, the boys would be racing head-long down the pier and into the lake while red-faced Mr. Tinker, his pants soaked to the waist, blew his whistle like he was trying to stop a train. "You motherfuther . . ." Mike shouted as Ricardo jumped in on top of him, but the rest of the words were lost in the splashing until I heard Walrus yelling from the shallow water, where he was coming full speed at me like a battleship: "There he is. There's Turd Head!"

So I'd dive deeper and pray that he wouldn't find me.

I tried to tell Mike how scared I was of his brother, but he wouldn't listen to any of that. "Grow up," he'd say. "Get real." Until the day when even he started to get spooked.

"We're in for some trouble," he said. "My brother's batteries are getting weak."

At first I didn't know what he meant, but I had noticed Walrus acting funny. From my tree behind the gymnasium I had seen him kicking along in the grass, fooling with the knobs on his radio and making low, awful sounds to himself. It was not the first time I had wondered why Walrus was the only boy at the school allowed to have a radio. None of the other boys would get near him now. When Mike tagged after him, Walrus shoved him away.

"Just remember to stay clear if anything happens," Mike said, but I didn't need to be warned.

During the next bingo game, just after Mr. Tinker had called out "B-4," Walrus bellowed and reared out of his chair, turning the table and all our bingo cards and chips onto the floor. Mr. Tinker ordered him to sit back down, but he didn't appear to hear. When one of the midgets touched his elbow, Walrus kicked him across the floor. Then he lumbered out of the dining room and down the aisle of our sleeping bay, turning footlockers upside down and ripping pillows apart with his hands.

"Stop him!" Mr. Tinker shouted. "Some of you boys stop him!" But we were all too terrified to move, so Mr. Tinker finally took a running start and tackled Walrus from behind. They hit the floor like sacks of feed.

While Mr. Tinker strained and clawed to keep Walrus down, Nurse Barmore tried to feel his pulse. He socked her in the nose, and she smiled sickly as the blood dripped onto her white blouse.

"Where's his radio?" Mr. Tinker panted. "Ricardo, find that radio! You, Mike, there's some batteries in the middle drawer of my desk. Get to it. Get to it!"

Then Mr. Tinker's wild eyes fell on me. "Can you sing, Lucius?"

I stared at him.

"I said *sing.*" Walrus tossed his head and snapped ferociously at something invisible in the air, and Mr. Tinker kicked me with his free foot. "Sing, dammit!"

I don't remember having learned the words, but before I knew it, I had launched into one of Miss Cooley's favorite songs, "Blue Velvet." I must have heard her sing it twice a day for as long as I could remember. Mr. Tinker nodded desperately, so I took a deep breath and kept it up. Walrus's eyes rolled, but he had stopped fighting Mr. Tinker's grip.

When I ran out of "Blue Velvet," I tried a little of "Looking Through the Eyes of Love" until it got too high and I had to switch to "April Love." Mike and

Ricardo were slow getting back with the radio and batteries, and by that time Walrus had gone completely limp. Mr. Tinker replaced the batteries and nestled the radio into Walrus's hand as easily as you might slip a rattle into a sleeping baby's fist.

"How'd you get him quiet?" Mike kept asking.

Then Walrus opened his eyes and spoke to me for the first time since I'd seen him behind the chain link fence. "Wait a minute," he said very solemnly. "I know what it is you look like. A lizard."

"Lizard," Mike repeated with a smile, and the idea tickled me.

"Meet me where they keep the brooms," Mike whispered that very next night.

Opening the closet door, I recognized the smell of orange juice and knew he was already there. "What's up?" I asked, brushing a mop strand from my face.

"You don't know?"

I felt trapped by the darkness.

"You don't know about my daddy's money?"

"No," I said.

"I've told you a million times. He's sending me some. To get away with."

"When you going?" I asked.

"*We*'re going! You and me and Walrus. Look. . . ." I heard paper unfolding. "I got a bus schedule."

"You can't read it in here," I said. "It's too dark."

"Don't matter. I got it memorized. They leave for Lake Charles every hour and a half."

"Walrus wouldn't mind me going?"

Mike grabbed me by the shirt. "We're gonna live on our boat. We'll fish and swim all day long."

"Is this something you're making up?" I said.

He pushed me away, and there was a long silence in the closet. "I don't never make things up," Mike finally answered in a low voice. "I did this plenty of times before you were around. I've been to Galveston. I danced naked with a whore in the middle of the street. You'll see what I'm talking about. As soon as the money's here, we're off." He laughed a weak laugh that trailed off in a cough. "You got to promise you'll go with us, Lizard. Promise?"

I did think about it. I thought about it all that night and the rest of the next day, about the fine threesome me and Mike and Walrus would make, strolling down the beach at Lake Charles.

To keep me interested Mike brought me pictures he said he'd found on his daddy's boat. They were of men and women screwing, but with their eyes blacked out. I wondered why their eyes were covered instead of their other things, which were in plain view. But the pictures gave me something to think about in the shower, and I got a kick out of watching Mike rock back and forth on his bunk, pointing at one picture or another and laughing until his eyes watered.

Mike said he had a girlfriend like the one in the pictures. When we got to Lake Charles, she'd do something special for me too. Then he said the people in the pictures had it all wrong, and he'd turn them upside down and say this was the way he and his girlfriend did it.

"What's this girl's name?" I asked.

"Rosa Lee," Mike said, kissing the tips of his fingers. "All you have to do is catch that bus. An hour and we'll be in Lake Charles. You and me . . . and Rosa Lee!"

* * *

But then some things happened that changed all that. "On Saturday night," Mr. Tinker told us after supper, "you're going to see a play. Provided you behave yourselves. You'll march to the gym single file, keep your mouths shut, and clap your hands at the end whether you enjoyed it or not."

The Friday before the play we broke up bingo early. A midget said the actors were spending the night in the parking lot, so Ricardo sneaked out to investigate. I lay on my bunk and watched the sky turn purple outside the nearest window. I had never seen a play, but I knew what one was. Miss Cooley had told me about the Christmas play she'd been in at the De Ridder First Holiness Church. She even draped a blue towel over her head and showed me the expression she made when Gabriel gave her the good news.

Miss Cooley might have been anywhere by then. Her last letter had come from Alexandria, Louisiana. It didn't make me sad. It just made me think for a minute about the places I didn't know about, the people I'd never met, about how wide the sky must be above the prairie, like pictures I'd seen in magazines, how the Mississippi River was over a thousand miles long. There were supposed to be lizards in Arizona as big as my leg, and Miss Cooley had told me about eagles who flew downriver in winter because the water up north was frozen and they couldn't find anything to eat. I thought about how I'd never slept out in the woods or seen a real deer. I hadn't been farther north than Shreveport or farther west than the Texas line. I didn't know anything about anything, I thought, as the sky outside my window turned black.

Then a shadow fell across my face. Mike breathed orange juice into my ear. "My daddy's money is coming soon." I nodded and fell into a sleep so light that orange juice was the first thing I smelled when I woke up.

"I saw them," Ricardo was saying as he waved his flashlight from ceiling to floor. "With a dog as big as a horse. They had on pajamas. I looked in the truck. There was a girl!" Then he took out his teeth and kissed them.

The other boys crowded around. "What'd she looked like?" they asked.

"What wheels!" Ricardo said.

Mike said, "I bet my girlfriend has better wheels."

"Your girlfriend," said one of the albinos.

"Yeah," Ricardo sneered. "Your girlfriend. . . ."

Mike rubbed his shriveled arm and gave me a knowing wink. *Rosa Lee.* He mouthed the words with satisfaction.

That Saturday came up warm and fresh-smelling. Everybody else went swimming at Alligator Lake, but I couldn't go because Ricardo had told Nurse Barmore I'd been playing with myself in the shower. So I wandered around the yard all morning, looking for snakes under rocks. I didn't find any, but I did see a black widow. It slinked out from under a coffee can. I watched it make its way over broken glass, gleaming black and mean. Then I turned it over with a stick so I could see its red mark. As I backed away, it righted itself on a blade of grass and disappeared under a brick.

The other boys came back early from swimming. They weren't hollering or cutting up. They hadn't even taken off their bathing suits. They just huddled in the parking lot, shivering, still wet.

"Lizard!" Ricardo called, but I didn't move.

"Come to the fence!" an albino motioned frantically.

I walked slowly toward them. "What is it?" I gripped

the fence, afraid they were going to pull something on me.

"You couldn't even recognize him," one of the albinos said.

"They was brothers, wasn't they?" said another.

"Where's Walrus?" I asked.

A midget grew excited, blubbering, "Quiet room, quiet . . . he bit the ambulance driver on the knee!"

"Look, Lizard," Ricardo began, his face so twisted, I thought he was going to spit at me.

"I saw it happen," argued the boy without any hands.

Suddenly it was quiet. Ricardo's bathing suit was so wet, a puddle had formed on the asphalt beneath him. His teeth were out, his lips were blue, and I could barely understand him when he finally said, "Mike got drowned."

But I didn't for one minute believe him.

2

THE FAR WALL of the gym had been painted to look like the inside of a tavern. There was a bar with rows of bottles, two tables with checkered cloths, and a real horseshoe above the locker-room door. While we scrambled for chairs, Nurse Barmore played "Blow the Man Down" over and over on the piano. One of the keys kept sticking. When she finally stopped, the lights went out. The boys raised the roof until they came on again. By then Nurse Barmore had started a different song, and from the locker-room door jumped a blond-haired boy and an old man who were carrying trays with mugs on them. They did a dance that was funny because they had to keep the mugs from spilling. At the end of the dance the boy took a bow and, sure enough, spilled everything on the old man. The old man kicked him in the seat of the pants, and I heard Ricardo's whinnying laugh above the others.

The boy shrugged his shoulders. "I am your servant

Jim Hawkins," he said, "and I have seen a world of woes." From the locker room staggered the old man in a different hat and with a scar down his cheek. "This is where it all began," Jim Hawkins whispered to us. "That's Bill, the Old Sea Dog." The Old Sea Dog stumbled around, carrying on about gold and bottles of rum. Then he fell down dead, a knife sticking out of his back.

Next Jim Hawkins was on a ship. He was being chased by Long John Silver, a horrible-looking old man with one leg. Jim Hawkins did everything he could to get away. He leapt into the aisle, did a cartwheel and then a somersault, and stood on his hands like a monkey. When Long John Silver tried to hit him with a chair, Jim did a backward flip, landing with his feet stretched out. But Long John Silver finally caught him, tied him up, and said he'd blow Jim's head off if he didn't tell the truth.

Jim Hawkins said, "Don't hurt me. I'll tell you everything. The treasure is buried on a place called Treasure Island!"

Long John Silver pointed his gun closer. "Where exactly is this Treasure Island, you filthy boy?"

"It's at the farthest edge of the ocean," Jim said.

"Ho-ho!" cried Long John Silver. "That's all I wanted to know, mate." Then he stuck the barrel of his gun next to Jim Hawkins's head.

The lights went out. I thought I heard a gunshot and the laughter of pirates. I jumped out of my chair, staring hard into the darkness, but when the lights came back on, there was nothing in front of me but an empty floor.

I tried to get back to the locker room so I could make sure Jim Hawkins was all right. There was a curtain in front of the door, and Nurse Barmore stood guarding the way.

"You won't find anything back here, Lucius. Get your Kool-Aid and find your seat."

A dog barked behind the curtain. "Go on, now," Nurse Barmore said when she saw me dawdling. But the sound of a scuffle in the gym got her attention, and in that moment when she wasn't looking, I drew the curtain back.

"Hush, Mac," a voice said.

Long John Silver was sitting on the floor in front of the lockers. Across from him Jim Hawkins sat backwards in a chair, one hand holding a book, the other hand stroking the back of a square-headed brown dog. "Try it again," Jim Hawkins said.

Long John Silver looked at the ceiling and began to recite: " 'The fringèd curtains of thine eye advance, and say what thou seest yond.' "

" 'What is't?' " Jim Hawkins read. " 'A spirit? Lord, how it looks about! Believe me, sir, it carries a brave form. But 'tis a spirit.' "

" 'No, wench; it eats and sleeps.' Okay, I've got that part," said Long John Silver. "Try it farther along. The temple line."

"Where?"

"There's nothing bad . . ."

"Oh, I know. 'There's nothing ill can dwell in such a temple.' " When Jim Hawkins said this, he looked straight up at me. He was tanned and had red cheeks. I could see the pencil lines around his eyes and the pure white where the makeup ended on his hands. He was so close, I could hear the in and out of his breathing. And his eyes, large, sad, as blue as Miss Cooley's, were fixed on me with the same surprise that was on Miss Cooley's face when she heard that angel in the Christmas play.

Then it hit me. Jim Hawkins was a girl, the girl Ricardo had seen in the parking lot. I let the curtain fall and didn't breathe, afraid to believe that she had been looking at me like that.

I worked fast that night. I wasn't sure how long it would take them to get their stuff put away in their truck, but I knew I'd have to hurry, before the other boys got settled for the night. I stuffed my clothes and toothbrush in the overnight bag and sneaked across to the quiet room. Walrus's hands were beneath the bars, his fingers white and square against the tile.

"I bet Mike's already in Lake Charles," I said.

Walrus stared at the tile without a word.

"I'm going too," I said. "We'll be waiting for you there."

Walrus opened his huge mouth but didn't speak. Instead, he crammed his fingers inside and bit down hard until the veins in his head stood out.

I backed away from the quiet room, out of the state school and into the night. Outside, the swallows were diving. It had started to rain. In the parking lot the actors were slamming their truck doors shut. I stepped out under a streetlight.

"Good God," the driver said.

"What is it?" It was the girl's voice.

"He just startled me, that's all." The driver clenched and unclenched his hands on the steering wheel. His cheeks were still splotched with makeup, and his hair stuck straight up in back like a kingfisher's feathers.

"Ask him what he wants, Cal," she said.

"What do you want?" the driver repeated.

I watched the girl lean forward against the dash. I

started to smile, but she glanced away. She wasn't a girl at all, not without the red cheeks and penciled eyebrows. She must have been in her twenties, a grown woman, and her mouth was thinner than it had looked in the gym.

"I want to go with y'all," I said.

"What'd he say?"

"He wants to go with us," the driver replied.

The woman sat back in her seat. The drizzle was cold on my neck, and I knew what was going to happen. "I can sing," I added.

The driver leaned his head out the window. "Get back where you belong before somebody misses you," he said softly. "Run on, now."

The next morning the sky stretched away like a white sheet. They had the funeral service for Mike in the gymnasium. While Nurse Barmore played "Jesus Is Calling," I walked down the aisle to pay my last respects. The casket looked heavy and deep, and thinking that Mike was way down at the bottom, I stuck my head all the way in. My nose touched something dry and cold, and jumping back, I saw his swollen blue face.

That afternoon a postcard came from Miss Cooley. It was postmarked Alexandria, Gateway to the Kisatchie National Forest. In the foreground was an Indian chief with his arms folded. In the background were straight white trees like I'd never seen before and a lake bluer than Miss Cooley's eyes. *Dear Lucius,* she began. *Having a good time?*

3

"LUCIUS, your father's here to see you."

I looked at Nurse Barmore with first one eye and then the other. "Who?"

"Your dad. D-a-d. Now get dressed quick. Take a shower first too. You stink." She continued to wrap the bandage around Ricardo's knee. One of the midgets had bit him in a fight over the name of a baseball team.

"My daddy's dead," I said.

"Don't tell *him* that."

"I don't want to go," I said.

"That doesn't matter, just get!" She ripped the bandage with her teeth.

It was too late. I was already running down the length of the sleeping bay, past the quiet room, and into the yard behind the school. When I got to my tree by the gymnasium, I didn't stop at the bottom, but wrapped my arms and legs around the trunk and shinnied up until I could take hold of the lowest branch. Then I swung on over, got my footing, and climbed two branches higher, made myself as small as possible, and calculated my chances of not being seen.

Below me I could see Walrus. He hadn't spoken to anybody since the day Mike had drowned. His radio had disappeared. Every day he just stood by the fence, gripping the wire with his stubby, raw fingers and staring off past the last line of trees.

"Lucius! Lucius!" Nurse Barmore called. She emerged to my left by the fence, looking squat like a fat white hen. "Get your fingers out of your mouth," she said to Walrus. "Have you seen that boy with the squashed head?"

I wanted to shout, Come on up here and get me if you can! But she circled the yard and was gone before I had the chance.

There was a light breeze and clouds, but it didn't look like rain. I figured I could last till dark, but I had the feeling then that somebody was looking at me. I turned to check it out, and there were two men by the incinerator at the edge of the parking lot—Mr. Tinker and a long-nosed guy with glasses and a mustache. They'd spotted me. The man with glasses put his hand on Mr. Tinker's chest as if to tell him to stay put, and then he started walking alone toward my tree. One thing was for certain. He wasn't dead.

"Lucius?"

I looked straight down, and he stared up at me, his bushy eyebrows cocked as though he'd heard a sound. His mustache almost completely covered his mouth. "You don't know me. My name is Simonetti. George Simonetti, from Brookline, Massachusetts. Can you hear me up there?"

"No," I said.

Simonetti reddened. I don't know why I had worried about him. My daddy would never have come from a place like Massachusetts. "I don't know what they've told you about me," Simonetti said. "Mr. Tinker and I just want to talk to you."

"Nurse Barmore says you're my dad. What would make her want to lie like that?"

"Is that what she said?" He stripped the leaves from a twig and let them settle to the ground. "Actually, we're not sure about anything. That's why we want to talk to you. See, I'm just a regular guy. I'm a shoe salesman. Drove here from Massachusetts. I'm on nobody's payroll but my own. Just checking things out. Why don't you come on down?"

"I like it up here."

"I can see that. But let me shoot straight with you, Lucius. I don't know whether anything will come of this, but I may be the only chance you'll have to get out of here."

I stared straight ahead like I wasn't impressed. After a while I heard Simonetti turn and walk back toward the parking lot. He was up to something. I knew that. At the same time I figured I'd better check him out. "Hey, mister!" I hollered. "I'm coming down."

Mr. Simonetti asked if he could smoke. When Mr. Tinker nodded, Simonetti reached inside his plaid sport coat and brought out a long cigar wrapped in gold foil. After peeling away the foil and clenching the cigar between his teeth, he lit it with a match and took a few short puffs to keep it going.

Mr. Tinker tapped his thick fingers on the desk. "Let's

get to the point of this," he said. "Mr. Simonetti claims
he's your father, Lucius. What do you think of that?" I
looked at the floor. "Well, I'll tell you what I think," Mr.
Tinker continued. "I think it's bull, but I'm letting him
talk to you because I don't believe in lawyers."

"Who said anything about lawyers?" Simonetti asked,
waving the smoke away.

"I did. And I don't like 'em." Mr. Tinker flipped open
a file on his desk and studied it for a minute, his large
white hands crossed like paws. "Lucius, I want you to
think very carefully and tell me the truth. A woman
named Cooley signed your papers. She any relation?"

"I don't know," I said.

Mr. Tinker's mouth turned up on one side in what
could have been a smile. "That's strange, isn't it?" He
waited like he expected me to answer. Then: "You lived
with her, didn't you?"

I nodded.

"But you don't know whether you're related to her?"

I shook my head.

"Did she ever mention Mr. Simonetti to you?"

"No."

"Did anybody?"

I shook my head.

"What's your dad's name, then?" I didn't answer him.
He licked a piece of spit off his upper lip, which was
arched and puffy like a woman's. "You don't know your
own dad's name?" He motioned Simonetti to stay put.
"Didn't you ever ask?"

"Stop badgering the boy," Simonetti finally said.
"He's told you what he knows."

Mr. Tinker slowly flipped the file closed, all the time

watching Simonetti with suspicion and dislike. "I'm just trying to jog his memory. He's retarded, you know."

"He doesn't look retarded to me," Simonetti said.

A lazy smile spread over Mr. Tinker's face. "I'd say the way he looks is a dead giveaway." I studied Mr. Tinker's office while he went on to list all the tests they had given me when I arrived at the school. He counted them up on his thick white fingers. The only tests I remembered were pissing in a bottle and putting blocks into holes, but I didn't say anything because I was just then trying to figure out a picture in the bookcase behind his head. Two men were kneeling on the ground with a woman's face between them, but then I realized the face was the head of a deer, and that she was dead. The men, one of them Mr. Tinker, were wearing Bermuda shorts and sunglasses. They were grinning like cats.

"The first we heard of him," Mr. Tinker was saying, "this Cooley woman shows up at our door with her fiancé, name of Alton Broussard. She signed the papers. It's legal as can be. Tell the truth, I feel sorry for the boy. The disfigurement could be genetic or the result of trauma at birth. We can never be sure which." Mr. Tinker's eyelids were nearly closed, as though he had memorized what he had said. He got up out of his leather chair, tapped the file on his desk. "Any questions so far?" Nobody said anything. "In that case, I'll be right back." He left, and the sound of his footsteps echoed down the hall.

Mr. Simonetti blew a smoke ring. "You okay?" he said.

I looked at him with first one eye and then the other. "What are you doing here?"

"That's a long story," he said, "but you have a right to know." He leaned back in his chair and watched the cigar smoke curl toward the ceiling. "A number of years ago I was stationed right here at Fort Polk. It was called Camp Polk then. I met a lady at a bar. She was a good woman, Lucius." He waited. "I loved her, wanted to marry her. But the plans we made never came through. I got transferred to Fort Dix in New Jersey, which was closer to my home. I never got back this way." He picked pieces of tobacco from his tongue. "Then some months later, the lady sent me news that she'd had a little boy and that . . . well, she gave me enough information that I figured I might know the boy if I ever saw him. But I never did. I'm not a particularly bad person, Lucius. I was just young and in the Army. When I got out, I married somebody up East. The years passed. We never had children ourselves, and my wife, God rest her soul, had a stroke one day. She was hoeing in her garden, in her thirties. It was a terrible thing. I found myself alone, a shoe salesman living in a little house on an inlet near the town." He looked down at his own shoes, as though to check the fit. "I was lonely," he said. "That was the thing. I was lonely. I started thinking about this lady in Louisiana and the boy she claimed was mine. So I came down here looking, asking questions. The answers I got led me here."

"Do you really think you're my dad?" I asked.

"I don't know. But if I am," he said as Mr. Tinker walked in, "you won't have to stay in this lousy place."

"We'll see about that," Mr. Tinker said. "I'm going to be asking some questions myself. Lucius, you go on back now."

"When can I see him again?" Simonetti asked.

Mr. Tinker spread his fat fingers on the desk. "The boys are going to the Fourth of July picnic tomorrow at Alligator Lake. If you want to chaperon, that's fine with me, although I hope you know what you'd be getting into."

"I don't mind. I don't have any plans for the Fourth anyway. What about you?" Mr. Simonetti asked me. "Do you mind if I tag along?"

I knew he had something up his sleeve, and for a minute there I thought I recognized him or that I'd seen somebody that looked an awful lot like him. "I don't care," I said.

Ricardo stopped pacing the aisle at Walrus's seat. "One more time, fat boy, and I'll knock that last tooth out of your head!" Walrus didn't seem to care. He tried to trip Ricardo again as the bus rocked down the road toward Alligator Lake.

I checked beside me to see what Mr. Simonetti would do, but he couldn't have seen Ricardo and Walrus even if he had wanted to. The albinos from the seat behind us had decided they liked him and were coiling around his neck and kissing him on both cheeks. Simonetti's glasses fogged with their breath as he tried to untwine them from himself and coax them to look out the window instead, where the barracks, firing ranges, and piney swamps of Fort Polk whizzed by under a shimmer of heat.

The bus slowed for some soldiers running in time along the shoulder of the road. They sweated through their green fatigues. The other boys pounded on the windows and rocked up and down in their seats.

"Boys, boys," Mr. Simonetti said, unplastering the albinos' arms from around his neck. He was wearing a pair of binoculars he said I could watch the fireworks with. He got so tangled up in the straps, I thought he might strangle himself.

Ricardo, meanwhile, had stopped in the aisle by our seats. "You talking to me?" he asked Simonetti. The albinos shrank back in terror.

"No, no, only to these fellows behind me." Simonetti grinned.

"If you think you see something funny," Ricardo said, "you better think again, or you'll be kissing your pearly whites good-bye just like me." Ricardo took out his teeth and kissed them, and Mr. Simonetti's face went pale.

"Don't let him bother you," I said as Ricardo sauntered toward the front of the bus. "He does that all the time."

"For a minute I thought they were real," Simonetti said, letting out his breath. "I guess I'm a little old for practical jokes. Never liked them much, anyway, to tell you the truth. Life's too much of a practical joke as it is." Something out the window caught his attention. "That's where I stayed, Lucius. Right there in Company B. I was twenty then. Of course, I did my advanced training up at North Fort. That's where I was when I met that lady I was telling you about."

I thought about it for a minute before I said, "You must be a lot younger than you look."

"Why's that?"

"If you met this lady when you were twenty." I searched his face. "I'm only thirteen."

"Oh, I see what you mean," he said, fingering the binocular straps. "You see, I knew her for a while. I was in the Army ten years. Didn't I tell you that? Worked my way up to E-7. Sergeant Simonetti. You should have heard those recruits try to say it. If they didn't get it right to the last syllable, they'd have to knock out fifty." He clicked his tongue like he was remembering those days with fondness and regret. "But what about you?" he asked. "I want to know more about you."

"You're lying to me," I told him straight.

Simonetti took a breath and looked hard out the window. His mustache raveled at the corners while he thought. "I don't intend to lie to you. My memory's just not as good as it used to be. But if I don't tell you everything about myself just yet, it's because I'm feeling you out, and I expect you to do the same." He smoothed the corner of this mustache with his hand.

The bus was slowing to a stop under the pines at Alligator Lake.

Simonetti bought me Sno-Kones, hot dogs with nothing but mustard, and peanuts roasted in the shell. A dozen politicians and officers made speeches, including a four-star general, but the loudspeakers weren't working right, so nobody could hear him anyway. Instead, Simonetti told me Army stories while we sat on a blue quilt at the edge of the lake. There must have five hundred other people there—soldiers and their families, the high-school band from Leesville in purple and gold, and busloads of kids from the regular schools, all dazzled by the heat. He used to sneak out of his barracks at night and fish Alligator Lake with a hand line. He told me how quiet it was in the morning when the soldiers were camped in the field, how much he liked it then, being out in the woods among men. "We should go camping together sometime," he said.

"Were you ever in a war?" I asked when he stopped long enough for me to get a question in.

"There was a war going on, but I didn't have to go to it, Lizard." I had told him to call me that. "I suppose I ought to be glad. But when I think of all the guys who did have to go and who had to lose their lives or come home injured, I feel guilty."

"Why? It wasn't your fault."

"War's everybody's fault," he said. He squinted through his glasses. "And everybody feels guilty about it. If you weren't in the Army, you feel guilty because you think of the guys who were. If you were in the Army, but didn't go to the war, you feel guilty because of the guys who went. If you went to the war and didn't get shot at, you feel guilty because of the guys who did. And if you got shot at, but survived, you feel guilty about the guys who died. I guess the only way you don't feel guilty is if you're dead. Now, that's some predicament, isn't it?"

He had lost me a long time ago. I nodded my head like I agreed, when all I was really doing was staring across Alligator Lake, watching for turtle heads.

"Is that one of the boys from the school?" Mr. Simonetti asked.

I looked where he was pointing and saw Ricardo standing over an officer and his family—a dumpy wife in sunglasses and two skinny kids. "What's he doing?" Simonetti asked.

I didn't want to guess. Ricardo had his hands on his hips and he was switching his ass like he always did when he told somebody off. Suddenly the officer stood up and slapped Ricardo in the face so hard, it sent him sprawling in the grass. A groan went up from the other families as though they were dreading what might come next, and before I knew he was gone, Mr. Simonetti was wading through them to the spot where Ricardo had disappeared in the grass. I jumped up and ran after him.

Mr. Simonetti was bent over trying to pull Ricardo up,

and the officer, a high-waisted little man with red hairs twisting from the back of his hands, was tugging from behind at Simonetti's shirt.

"Let me have that little son of a bitch!" the officer wheezed in a thin voice. "I'll kill the little son of a bitch!" Ricardo was giggling so hard, Mr. Simonetti couldn't get him to sit up, so he turned and asked the officer just what was going on.

"Who the hell are you?" the officer wheezed.

"I'm a shoe salesman from Massachusetts. The name's Simonetti."

"Is that some kind of joke?" the officer said. "I've seen you around here before."

"Not me. You must be confusing me with someone else. I drove in day before yesterday. Now, why'd you hit the boy?"

"Why? I'll tell you why. He was making lewd remarks to my wife."

"She's the best piece I've ever had!" Ricardo shouted from the grass, and Mr. Simonetti had to restrain the officer with both hands.

"Hold it, hold it," Mr. Simonetti said. "The boy's not in his right mind. He doesn't mean to say the things he says."

"Get your hands off me!" the officer gasped.

"She a little dry at first," Ricardo said, sitting up, "but in a little while, man oh man . . ."

The officer struggled again with Mr. Simonetti, and I looked at his wife to see how she was taking all this. She popped her gum and then reached over to slap one of her skinny kids on the leg.

"Look, he's from the state school," Mr. Simonetti said. "He doesn't know what he's saying."

"Oh, yeah?"

"He's retarded and emotionally disturbed."

"A retard, huh?" the officer said.

Simonetti let go of the officer's coat. "I knew you'd understand. Now let's just try to forget this. I'll get the boy back to the bus. He won't bother you again."

— The officer looked confused and rumpled. "Well, I want an apology first. Nobody says things like that to my wife. I don't care how screwed up they are in the head."

"All right." Mr. Simonetti sighed. He turned to the woman and her kids. "I'm sorry about what this young boy has been saying. It won't happen again." The officer's wife wrinkled her nose at him and then grinned.

The officer turned red. "I want *him* to say it," he wheezed. "Let him say his *own* apologies."

Mr. Simonetti slowly shook his head. He took the officer by the shoulder and, in a low voice, said, "Don't press your luck with this one, sir. He killed a state trooper last year with his bare hands."

The officer's chin dropped, and the blood left his face. "Candy, let's move to the other side of the lake. Hurry up now," he said. And then he saw me. "Is this another one of them? Goodness, you'd think a decent family could have a picnic without having to look at deformed children all day."

"That's enough, mister," Simonetti said. And Ricardo suddenly jumped up and ran for the bus, shouting, "She charged me two dollars, then gave me the clap!"

"Candy, don't listen to that filth!" the officer said. Then he squinted at Simonetti. "Wait a minute. I remember you now. You were in training here."

"Years ago," Simonetti said. "I was here before you were even out of ROTC."

"I wasn't in ROTC," the officer wheezed, as if that proved everything.

"Come on, Lizard," Mr. Simonetti said.

He and the driver locked Ricardo in the bus and stationed the albinos there as guards. That suited them fine. They weren't allowed in the sun anyway and had been playing hide-and-seek all day underneath the trees.

Toward dusk Mr. Simonetti moved the blue quilt to the end of the lake by the dam, where he said we would get a better view of the fireworks. The air was completely still. Occasionally a baby would cry or somebody would set off a cherry bomb deep in the woods, but for the most part the picnic was over. Everybody looked wilted from the sun, heavy with food, and worn out from keeping the kids in line all afternoon. Mr. Simonetti and I were quiet, watching the water turn soft gray like the sky. If I stared long enough, the surface of the lake dropped away, and it seemed like I was high above a field of snow surrounded by pointed trees.

"What really makes you think you're my dad?" I finally asked him.

"It's like I told you," he said. I couldn't see his eyes, for his glasses had turned gray like the lake. "I knew this lady friend of mine had had a boy your age. When my wife died, I came here looking. I was lonely. My life had petered out. It hits you hard when your car's paid for but you don't have anyplace to go. So I checked around in De Quincy and found somebody who had known my friend, but she'd left there a long time ago. They said the boy might be in the state school."

"I grew up in De Ridder, not De Quincy."

"That's what I said." His mustache quivered. "Well,

what difference does it make?" he asked, looking over my shoulder. "The point is, I think you're my boy."

"You don't really think that," I said. "And I'll tell you something else. You may have been in the Army once. But you never had any lady friend around here."

He looked me in the eye. His nose was like a dinner roll. "What makes you say that?"

"Because if you'd known a woman from here and you were really lonely, you'd be trying to track her down instead of me."

The first rocket sounded like a thunderclap. From every corner of the lake women screamed. The rocket flashed once in the air above a twisted plume of smoke, then boomed again louder, and it was dark. A dud, the crowd seemed to moan. I looked back toward the bus and wondered whether the albinos would wet their pants like they had at the rodeo.

It sounded like thunder again, and this time the rocket rose with a hiss, leaving a sparkling trail as thin as an eyelash. There was a pause, a flash of light, and the sky above us opened in green and yellow that showered onto the lake.

"Did you see that?" Simonetti asked.

"I've seen fireworks before," I said, although I hadn't. The air smelled dangerous and sharp. "Over there!" cried boys in the field beyond the lake, their flashlights red in the rolling smoke. They were setting off an entire row, and suddenly the sky rattled with little explosions leading to a huge gold and silver ball that collapsed upon itself.

"What was this lady's name, anyway?" I asked.

"I'll tell you later. Did you see those spinning things?"

Two rockets crossed paths. They exploded like starfish, one on top of the other. For the first time I noticed the sirens and, beneath them, the sound of the Leesville High School Band tuning up. A trombone made a sliding note as another dud fell tumbling into the water. Then the band struck up "Oh, say, can you see . . ." and after a minute people started to sing. It sounded like wind through trees. The rockets came closer together now, a blue one, then crimson and gold, and green. The band and voices went higher, off key, until the field beyond the lake started hissing and sputtering brightly through the smoke. "Take cover!" the boys cried, their flashlights bobbing, and a dozen or more rockets went up all at once. I knew what was coming: "The land of the free . . ." but I'd had it with Simonetti's lies.

"What do you really want out of me?" I said.

He turned just enough so that the whole lit-up sky was reflected in his glasses. "All right, Lizard," he replied. "You win." He peeled off his mustache and rolled the tip of his nose into a little ball. "There's nothing to be afraid of." He took off his glasses and turned fully to face me.

They were singing, "The home of the brave." I didn't recognize him for a minute, until the play about Treasure Island came back to me. He was Long John Silver, and in the dead silence after the fireworks had ended, I turned around, following his eyes. Parked beside the school bus, underneath the trees, was the actors' truck, its engine ticking, and the woman who had played Jim Hawkins was waiting for me.

4

THE REST OF that night seems like a dream to me now. After the fireworks we filed into the bus in the dark. Simonetti, or whatever his name was, counted heads by touch. The other boys seemed subdued. The fireworks had worn them out, or maybe they were just thinking about Mike. He had always had fun on the bus ride back from the lake. Simonetti and I sat together but didn't say much. The truck and the girl who had played Jim Hawkins were like secrets that we couldn't name without causing them to disappear.

Simonetti had put back on his false nose and mustache. He was wearing his glasses again. And when he said good-bye to the rest of the boys at the front gate, he winked at me. Nurse Barmore continued counting. She didn't appear to suspect a thing. He had already told me to sneak out to the back fence behind the incinerator at exactly eleven o'clock (he had loaned me his watch to make sure I wasn't late).

That night Walrus talked in his sleep. "Gimme that back!" he said. "Stop it!"

The boy without any hands snored like he always did. At five till eleven I pushed the sheet off and sat on the edge of my bed, fully dressed. I already had my overnight bag with my toothbrush and extra clothes in it. The moonlight fell from the high windows on the sleeping boys and Mike's empty bed.

Ricardo's bed was empty too. He was in the quiet room this time because of all the fuss he'd caused at Alligator Lake. I peeked through the bars before I went past. He was asleep sitting up in the corner, his mouth open. He'd left his false teeth in the soap dish, where they glimmered in the moonlight like fish.

Ricardo had showed us all how to disconnect the fire alarm, although nobody had had any reason to do it until now. I worked quickly and then pushed open the fire exit into the yard. The windows of the kitchen were lighted. I could hear the clink of metal trays. The cook's helpers did their baking at night, while everybody else slept. Everybody but Mr. Tinker. I don't think he ever slept, and I had to wait until I saw his flashlight disappear down the steps to the boiler room before I sprinted across the yard.

At the fence I was sure something had gone wrong. The actors' truck was nowhere to be seen. All I could hear was the sound of water trickling in the drainage ditch on the other side of the fence and the rubbery swish of distant cars on the road to Toledo Bend. Then suddenly I heard a tapping on the sidewalk across the street. It was an old woman taking her evening walk. She was bundled in sweaters and wore a scarf tied beneath her chin. When she saw me, she stopped and motioned with her cane. I thought at first she was telling me to get away from the fence, so I stepped back. No, no, her cane seemed to say. Come here. I knew I was in for it then. I stepped farther back into the shadows of my tree.

With what appeared to be a shrug, the old woman slowly crossed the street. Using her cane for balance, she stepped over the drainage ditch and put her face right up to the fence.

"Up and over," she said. "Throw your bag first, and be careful about the barbed wire." It was Simonetti.

And when I had scaled the fence, he helped me down the other side, and we crossed the drainage ditch and walked hand in hand down the sidewalk on the other side of the street. Two blocks away we came to a dead-end street where the truck sat running without lights, and I knew I was on my way.

I woke up that first morning with a view out the back of the truck, of blue sky and white clouds moving fast. The air smelled familiar, but I couldn't place it until we rounded a curve in the road, and I saw the rows of peach trees, little crooked things with dark leaves, trailing up one hill and down the other. Peach is my favorite ice cream.

"You awake?" a voice asked.

My eyes hadn't gotten used to the light, but I knew it was Jim Hawkins.

"Yes, ma'am," I said, staring hard in the direction of her voice. I wondered if any black widows might be nesting in the creases of the tarp that covered the truck bed.

"We didn't get far. Callahan got us lost."

"Is that Mr. Simonetti's real name?"

Now I could make out her silhouette against the flapping sides of the truck. She was sitting up and pulling a sleeping bag around her shoulders. "Could you hand me that box of Kleenex, please?" I found it behind a cardboard mask stapled to a stick. She wadded her piece of chewing gum in the Kleenex and sailed it out the back. It hung in the air, then dropped to the road and somersaulted away.

"I know they call you Lizard, but I've forgotten your real name."

"Lucius Sims. I'm from De Ridder."

"We're not far from there now," she said. "I'm Sallie Petrie, from Pine Bluff, Arkansas. And over there taking a snooze is Mac." Behind her I could see that square-headed dog curled around an open makeup kit.

"Didn't Callahan tell you? We're going to Alabama to do a play. It's about a shipwreck, and there's a part in it for you. Didn't he say anything about it?"

I shook my head.

"He's so scatterbrained."

"He said he was a shoe salesman from Massachusetts and that his wife had had a stroke."

Sallie smiled and shrugged off the sleeping bag. Her blouse was tied behind her neck and her shoulders were bare. "I bet he wouldn't get out of character long enough to tell you the truth."

"It doesn't matter," I said. "I wanted to go with y'all no matter what."

"I know," she said. "We talked about it all the way back to camp. You looked so determined, standing there in the rain. That's when we got the idea about the play. It seemed too good to be true. How do you like Mac?"

"A dog's a dog," I said.

"Not this one, Lizard. He's special. He won't do anything you ask." She smiled again, and about that time we stopped for gas.

I jumped out to take a leak, and when I came back, Mr. Simonetti, or Callahan, was leaning against the tailgate, tossing pieces of gravel into a muddy puddle while Mac sat on his haunches and watched.

I looked from Sallie to Callahan to Mac. Behind them the peach trees moved in the wind. We were going to have fun, the four of us. I knew that right off the bat.

Callahan said we'd been driving in circles. He and Sallie had two more performances of *Treasure Island* to do, one in the morning at the elementary school in Newllano, the other in the afternoon at the junior high, and they couldn't afford not to show up. His theory was to stay on the road during the day so as not to attract attention, and wait until dusk to find a place to camp. The towns we passed through were a lot like De Ridder, with trailer parks and lumberyards and unmarked railroad tracks. We drove slow when we hit a street with big houses, the daylilies bright in patches of sunlight, everything else cool and dark and green. The kids playing freeze tag on the grass squinted at us like they'd never seen a truck before.

When we passed a mileage sign for Newllano, Sallie said, "You don't know how much I dread having to do *Treasure Island* again."

"It's the last time," Callahan answered. "I promise. After that we don't stop till Vicksburg."

"That's what you said before Leesville."

"Well, it turned out all right, didn't it?" He looked at her. "We've got to get some cash somehow."

"I know. I'm not complaining. It's just crazy to be

hanging around here when they'll be looking for Lizard all over the place."

"That's the idea," Callahan said. "Fly into the face of the enemy. Pretend that you've nothing to hide. We're committed to do the play in Newllano. If we show up, we're above suspicion. We make some bucks. Everything works out fine. If we don't show up, we're broke, and people are talking about us."

"Okay," Sallie said. "We just need to keep track of where our money goes."

"That's what happens when you get old, Lizard."

What? I wanted to ask, but a change in Callahan's expression stopped me. He hit the brakes as we topped a hill and pulled off the highway into a patch of honey-suckle.

"What's wrong?" Sallie asked.

"The last car that passed us was blinking his lights. There's a speed trap ahead."

"So?"

"It could be a license check."

"Why don't we just turn back?" Sallie asked.

Callahan smiled. "I have a better idea. Both of you get in the back. Lizard, take off your clothes and curl up next to Mac. Sallie, put Mac's collar on Lizard and cover up his hands and feet. I'll take care of the rest."

"What are you going to do?" Sallie asked.

"I'm telling you, don't worry. Now, we've got to be quick."

Sallie and I did what he said. It was fun in a way, except that Mac wouldn't stop licking me in the face. Callahan pulled back onto the highway and coasted down the hill and around a curve before he began slowing down. When the truck stopped, we heard a voice say, "Morning. This is just routine. We're looking for a runaway from the Leesville State School. He's a deformed retard. You couldn't miss him if you tried."

"A boy?" Callahan replied.

"That's right. You seen him along the road?"

"Not that I recall."

But another voice said, "We better check the back."

"Feel free." Callahan's door opened, and we heard footsteps in the gravel along the road. "There's just my wife back here, tending to some pretty carsick dogs." Someone pulled the canvas flap back and the sunlight leapt in. A sheriff's deputy with cauliflower ears squinted inside.

"How are you, ma'am?" he said. "I'm sorry to disturb you."

"That's quite all right." Sallie's voice sounded husky. I pretended to be asleep.

"Take a look here, Homer," the deputy added. "That's the ugliest dog I've ever seen. What kind do you reckon he is?"

"Beats me."

"Short-haired, tailless Weinerrheiner," Callahan said. "He won the best of breed at the Lake Charles show."

"No kidding. Weinerrheiner? I've never heard of that one before. Did you get him around here?" the deputy asked.

"Nope, in Tupelo. He's an oddity. We picked him up for a song. If you'd like to see his sire, give me a call. My name's Simolinsky, in Rosepine. I'm in the book."

"Rosepine, huh? Well, I'll do that. My wife raises Pekingese. She'd get a kick out of this one. You say there's a long-haired variety too?"

Callahan let go of the flap, and Sallie took a deep

breath in the dark. "Yes, but they don't do too well in the climate around here." We heard them walking toward the front.

"I'm going to take you up on that now. My wife and I are through Rosepine all the time," the deputy said.

"Do that. We'd enjoy having you."

"Sorry to have held you up."

"No problem. It was good to meet you. And I hope you find that boy!" Callahan's door slammed shut and the truck started away.

"I'll be darned," Sallie said. "That Callahan."

He took us on back roads until late in the afternoon, then pulled onto the shoulder, killed the engine, and walked to the back. "We'll camp here tonight," he said. "Then tomorrow Sallie and I will drive back to Newllano. It's not a good idea for you to go with us. After the play we'll come back here to get you and then we'll be off for good. Right now, though, I need to take a break."

We unloaded the tent and set it up in a clearing not far from the road. Sallie unfolded a canvas-back chair and sat in the shade, going over her lines. Callahan found a stick and threw it into the brush. "Fetch it, Mac!" he shouted. Mac looked at him and then stretched out underneath a tree.

When night fell, Callahan built a fire. Mac and me went deep into the peach orchard to find wood. It was cool. The wind in the trees sent shivers across my forearm, and the stars when they popped out were bright as ice. While we stacked branches, Sallie heated beans and wieners over the fire. She walked barefoot and wore a loose robe tied at her waist. Her hair was still pinned in back except for one strand which kept getting in her way. For a minute, with the lights from the fire reddening her cheeks, she looked like she had in the play, wet lipped and young as me.

"Tomorrow we'll have rabbit," she said. "We trap our own and cook them fresh."

"They're good," Callahan said. "Sallie fries them in corn flour, with fresh tomatoes on the side."

We sat cross-legged around the fire, finishing the wieners and beans. "I should have set the traps out before it got dark. We'll just have to do it after we eat. Then tomorrow morning you'll need to check them. You think you can do it?"

"Sure," I said.

"You won't have to skin them or anything. Just bring them back here." Callahan forked the beans into his triangular face. "We'll be more civilized when we get to Birmingham."

I threw my paper plate into the fire and leaned back on my elbows while Sallie and Callahan talked softly about a number of things, about friends back in Houston where they lived and plays they'd been in together. They told stories on each other and looked for me to laugh about places and people I'd never seen. They wondered aloud about Birmingham. What was it like in the summer? Were there good people there? Any jazz? Sallie said she needed a secondhand clothing store. A lot depended on whether the theater people were serious or just doing the play for kicks. Yes, but Callahan hoped they liked to have a good time. Sallie said she wouldn't worry about that. Waldo was directing, wasn't he? Sure, there'd be some good times. And the theater was new, well, a newly renovated space anyway. They had spent a lot getting it into shape, and this was the first play in it. Here's hoping we get paid, Callahan said. We better, she laughed. You think Mac will adjust to the heat? You can't get hotter than Houston. I mean the humidity. Ask Mac, Callahan said. It doesn't matter to me where we are, as long as we're together. Isn't that the way the song goes? That's the way all the songs go, Sallie said. And their voices wove in and out and around each other, the comforting sound of grown-ups with nothing important to say.

"What does your real dad do for a living?" Sallie asked me.

"He's dead."

For a minute nobody broke the silence. "I'm sorry," Callahan finally said. "If I'd known, I never would have pulled that Simonetti routine. The records Mr. Tinker showed me didn't say anything about it. In fact . . ."

"What?"

"Your records just weren't complete, that's all." He flipped a twig into the fire. "Let's set out those traps so we can get to sleep." He scraped the leftovers on the ground for Mac, who woke long enough to eat. "Let's go, Mac," said Callahan, but it was too late. He had already fallen back to sleep.

"Don't go too far," Sallie said before we left.

The orchard was still and cold. It was the strangest weather for July I'd ever seen. The moon followed us for a distance and then slipped behind some clouds, but the walking was easy until we hit the real pine woods on the other side. I had to follow Callahan by the crashing sound he made through the brush. We came out into another orchard for a while and then dipped again into the pines. I wondered why we were going so far until Callahan stopped to let me catch up. "I'm looking for an open place with tall grass and weeds," he said. "You doing all right?"

I nodded and the moon came out again. It was hard getting used to Callahan's real face, which was narrow and pointed like a fox's.

When we got to a clearing, he stopped. We were by a stream that ran like silver into the mist and under the outline of an old pump house.

"This is just what I was looking for," Callahan said.

He untied the bright wire traps from his belt, staked them to the ground, and baited them with Brussels sprouts. Then he squatted in the tall grass and took a cigar from the pocket of his flannel shirt. I knelt beside him.

"I know I've got some explaining to do." He lit the cigar, and the flame fleshed out his face, made it glow like Simonetti's. "I should've just walked into that guy's office at the school and said, 'Look, I'm not this kid's father, but I'm taking him anyway. Show me where to sign.' So why didn't I? Time, for one. Nothing ever works out that easy. Second, Sallie and I couldn't take a kid right now. Nothing personal, Lizard, that's just the way things are. And secondly, or thirdly, you don't need anybody telling you what to do. Are you following me?"

I looked at him with first one eye and then the other.

"The point is—this is business. You wanted to go with us. All right, we got you a part at union scale. Jerry, the guy they originally cast, couldn't make it. He's drying out at the VA in Galveston. He wasn't right anyway. But you're perfect, assuming you can learn your lines and take directions. After the show and we get paid, you're on your own. If you want to go back to the school, that's fine, although you know you don't belong there."

"How much of what you're telling me is true?" I asked.

He took the cigar out of his mouth. "Jesus, Lizard, what do I have to do?" He shook his head. "Okay, Jerry's not in the hospital. Maybe he ought to be, but he's not. I just said that for dramatic effect."

"What?"

He waved me away. "Nothing. I was just trying to make a better story. There's no harm in that, is there?"

I thought about Mike and his story about Nurse Barmore's submachine gun.

"Well, do you think you can find your way back here in the morning to check the traps?" Callahan put out his cigar, saving the rest, and stood up. We looked at the traps, the stream, the pump house, through the mist. "The secret is to go straight from the truck through the campfire and into the orchard. If you get lost, you can follow the stream."

"Will we really catch rabbits?" I asked.

"I don't know." He shifted his weight while he listened. "There's something out here."

We ran into Mac on the way back out. He angled toward us with his broad head down and his tail beating the brush. Callahan patted him and ordered him back to the truck. Mac stretched but stayed in the orchard, snuffling under an overturned log.

"That took you long enough," Sallie said. "I got spooked." She was wrapped in her sleeping bag by the fire. "Kept hearing noises. You don't think those deputies are still around, do you?"

"No, it's probably just animals," Callahan said. "Armadillos rooting for grubs. Did you take a shower?"

"Yeah, I stuck my head under the water barrel and

dried my hair by the fire. It felt so good, Cal. Why do people live in cities?"

"Maybe so they won't hear noises in the woods. I think I'll wash up too. Here, Lizard." He threw me a Hershey bar from his shirt pocket. "I got it at the gas station and forgot. It's probably melted."

"That's all right," I said. "I like them that way." I stood by the fire, peeling the white wrapper away from the squares.

"You know," Sallie said, "your eyes are the prettiest green."

"Some people think I'm bad luck," I said. The trees in the orchard seemed to breathe, and the fire made a whistling sound. "My daddy died right before I was born. Last week my friend at the school got drowned. I've heard people say that I was a bad sign."

"Bull," she said. "Some people think everything's a sign, and a bad one at that. Do you ever hear anybody talking about good signs?" There was a string of blue beads around Sallie's neck, each bead lit with a flame from the fire.

"This play we're going to be in," I said. "What's it called?"

"It's *The Tempest,* by William Shakespeare. Ever heard of him?"

"Sort of," I said.

"He's really great. You're going to love it. It's a story about a magician and his daughter. They live on this island with a spirit named Ariel and the magician's slave. The magician causes a storm to wreck a ship carrying some of his enemies—am I boring you?"

"No, I was just thinking about snakes."

"Please don't talk about snakes," Sallie said.

"They won't hurt you."

"Lizard, I'm serious. Stop."

"They're pretty, Sallie. I'll find you one along the road."

"I'm telling you, stop."

But I knew she was having fun. "I had a king snake who sunbathed on my stomach." Sallie shuddered. "He'd put his head in my mouth."

"Shut up!"

I knelt beside her and whispered, "He slept with me."

She shook her head like it was full of bees. "God, Lizard, have some decency!"

I lay back in the grass. The stars whirled above my head. "How long have you known Callahan?" I asked.

"That's more like it," she said. "Five years in May."

"Do you trust him?"

"Sure. Don't you?"

"I don't know. Can I trust you?"

Sallie looked troubled. She pulled her sleeping bag closer.

5

THE NEXT morning I wandered into the peach orchard
on a line from the road through the campfire, just like
Callahan had told me to. He and Sallie had left for
Newllano right after breakfast, and he'd said they'd be
back to get me in the afternoon around three. The sun
wasn't up good, and I wished I had brought one of Callahan's flannel shirts. When I got out of sight of the place
where we had camped, I stopped and looked around me.
This wasn't just one big orchard, but a series of small
ones separated by stands of pine and sweet gum. I realized that this was the first time since I'd left De Ridder
that I'd been completely alone. If I'd wanted, I could
have taken off then, made my way to Highway 171, and
followed it to Lake Charles. But I figured the actors
would get me wherever I needed to go. In the meantime
I had food and a sleeping bag. And Sallie, who had
promised to tell me more about the magician and his
island. Right now, though, it felt good to be away from

the actors, smelling the overripe peaches and the bitter, clean pines.

Suddenly a fox appeared in the path. He had gray fur outlined in orange and a white chest that the sunlight touched in the shape of a wedge. He stood with one leg raised, his ear cocked, and I think he must have been listening then to the same sound I heard, a rustling through the brush like somebody was dragging a branch. The sound stopped, the fox looked at me like he'd known me before, in another life, and then, because the memories weren't so good, he vanished without making a sound or disturbing a single leaf.

I waited but didn't hear the dragging sound again. Perhaps it had been a lost calf or just crows—they make an awful lot of noise for their size. But to be on the safe side I skirted that stretch of pine and picked up again in the next orchard. Right away I found a stream, and remembering what Callahan had said, I followed it down a narrow gully until the sun disappeared and I was cold again.

At first I thought I might have been wrong to walk along the stream instead of keeping straight through the orchards and pine woods, but after about twenty minutes of dips and turns, I came to what must have been the pump house. It had a tin roof, windows on the two sides I could see, and walls that were buckled and splintered with age. The stream disappeared beneath it. From where I stood, it looked like squirrels had been trying to build nests in the windows. There was pine straw crammed above the sills, along with pieces of milk cartons and rags. What was more—on the bank of the stream somebody had set out a line of marigolds. Somebody lived in the pump house, although I didn't see how that could be.

"What'cha think you're doing?" a voice behind me said, and I felt my legs go weak. "Turn around slow," the voice said. "I got a shotgun, so don't act funny."

I turned the way I would if I'd had a book on my head, not daring to breathe. A black boy in boots, cutoff jeans, and a floppy hat stood staring at me. He didn't have a gun.

"Why'd you scare me like that?" I said. "I'm not doing anything."

"I just said I *had* a gun. I didn't say I had it with me. It's in the house. Yonder, you can look for yourself." In the nearest window I saw the black barrel protruding, although I couldn't tell who might be holding the other end.

"If you'll just let me find what I'm looking for, I'll be on my way," I said.

"And what might you be looking for, white boy? As if I didn't know. Who gave you permission to kill my rabbits? They're mine just like this land we're standing on. It was deeded to me by my great-great-grandfather, Chief Narrow Meadow. I'm full-blood Creek." He waited to let that bald-faced lie sink in. "How'd you come to be so ugly? Rain, come get a load of this boy here. He look like he from outer space." I heard a muffled answer from inside the pump house, but Rain, whatever or whoever that was, didn't appear.

"Is that gun in there loaded?"

"If it weren't, I'd be a fool to say so, wouldn't I?" the black boy replied. "I've learned a few tricks from my people, I can tell you that. Like how to make salamander pie and how to drink from the silver bowl. How to make a white boy wet his pants because he thinks he's fixing to get shot. I can work all kinds of magic, but the best thing I do is dance. Watch this, now, and don't make any funny moves." The black boy closed his eyes as though he were listening to an imaginary beat. "So fine," he sang with his chin thrust out. "My baby's so doggone fine."

"That's not an Indian dance," I said.

"Yeah? And how does a squash-headed white boy who hasn't been in these woods for five minutes know what is an Indian dance and what ain't?"

I couldn't help but smile.

"What's funny?" he said in a low, bitter voice, only inches from my face. "You think the whole damn country belongs to you, don't you? Well, I'm here to tell you it don't!

"Rain!" he suddenly yelled. "Come out here and get a load of this freak. There must be a circus around here, and this one escaped!"

"I can't right now, Sammy," a girl's voice sang. "The cornbread'll burn. Ask him inside to eat."

"To eat!" Sammy was indignant. "You want to share our food with this subhuman, humpbacked thing? If our great-great-grandfather was alive, he'd die. I swear he would." Sammy picked up a rock and zinged it low over the weeds until it rose above the peach trees and disappeared. "He was a chief. The bravest and most famous of the Creeks." Satisfied with himself, he turned back around. "Well, don't you want something to eat?"

I didn't know what to make of him, but I followed Sammy up the path to the pump house. The inside was dark and smelled like chicken frying, but also something sweet. The first place I looked was the window to check out the gun. It was a crowbar propped up in a chair. I didn't know what to believe.

Lining the walls were a couple of dozen water-snake skins, dried and tacked in place, all different sizes, but with the same saddle-shaped pattern and eyes that were clouded white. The skins gave off a sour, salty smell up close. Then I saw in the corner a portable butane stove painted green. It had U.S. ARMY written on the side and a serial number mostly worn away. And the girl standing in front of it with her back to me, poking at some frying meat, her dark hair in braids, and her darker skin visible between her shirt and jeans, must have been Rain.

Sammy took off his hat and said, "Make yourself at home, you wall-eyed excuse for a human being."

"Sammy," Rain said, "be kind. We haven't had a visitor in over a year. What if you were in the woods alone? Mama told us to always say our prayers and never refuse strangers something to eat."

" 'Mama, Mama,' that's all I hear around this place. I'd say Mama was a bit too generous, wouldn't you? Letting that one-eyed piece of—"

"I don't want to hear about it. You're enough to spoil an appetite." Rain turned and looked straight at me. "Forgive my brother." My heart dropped to my feet. Her skin was as smooth as an otter's back, and her eyes were large and clear. "Pull up a chair," she said. "I'm Rain."

"I'm Lucius Sims, but they call me Lizard."

"I bet I know how he got that name!" Sammy said.

"Sammy, go pick some berries and wash them in the stream. The rest of the food's about ready." She waited. "Go on now."

Sammy gave her a look, then slapped his hat on and left.

"Would you like a drink of water?" Rain asked. "It's from the stream." And she proceeded to dip a cup from a barrel by the stove. I looked around for a chair. There were two folding metal ones in the corner by the door, where a Coleman lantern sat on a stool and two rolled-up blankets hung from the wall above a shelf filled with books.

"Do you live alone?" I asked, unfolding the chair and sitting down.

"Most of the time. We like it here." She handed me the cup. "In the evenings fireflies light up the place. Deer sometimes drink at the stream. What about you? Where do you live?" She didn't sit, but crouched on the balls of her feet, hugging her legs and resting her chin on her knees.

"I'm an actor," I said.

"Really?"

"All my life," I said, and I was lying so much now, I had to get up and walk around, first to the door, where I could see Sammy bent in the bushes, singing softly to himself, and then to the window above the stove, where a blue jay sat on the low branch of a dogwood tree, cocking his head at me. "I'm on the road from Houston to Birmingham, where we're going to do a play. It's about a shipwreck on an island. I'm playing the lead," I said straight to the blue jay, daring him to say a thing.

"What's your name in the play?"

She'd got me there. Sallie hadn't told me yet. I pretended not to hear. "Are you and Sammy really Creeks?"

Rain thought about that for a minute. "Let's say we're what we look like, and we're something else that you can't see."

I took a long drink of water. "That goes for me too," I said.

"I wish Sammy and I could see your play."

"That would be great, but don't say anything to him just yet." He was scuffling up the path toward the pump house.

"You'll like Sammy when you get to know him," Rain said. She unfolded her arms and stood up, stretching as far as she could reach.

Sammy came in. "I got your damn berries, and I almost got my ass nibbled off in the process. Don't 'Mama' me no more, Rain."

"Did I say anything?" Rain was poking again at the frying meat.

Sammy set up a rusted card table by the window, I got the other chair and stool, and Rain brought the sizzling meat and served it on tin plates. "Rabbit!" I said, putting two and two together, but Sammy didn't say a thing. And Rain also brought hot cornbread, buttermilk, black-eyed peas, and yams, a salad with spring onions, radishes, and tender dandelion leaves. For dessert she showed me how to dip wild huckleberries in honey and dust them with brown sugar that she kept in a jar on the shelf. "They never had anything like this at the school," I said.

"What school?" Sammy glowered. "What have you two been talking about in here?"

"Nothing, Sammy." Rain touched his arm.

"Last one in's a one-eyed snake!" he said, bolting from the table and into the noonday heat.

"Sammy!" Rain called. "You better let your food digest."

We heard a splash from what must have been the stream.

"Twelve is a terrible age," she said. "He won't listen to a thing I say. You want to go for a swim?"

"I didn't bring anything to wear."

Rain's dark eyes danced. "Whoever heard of wearing something when you swim?"

"Catch me, Rain!" Sammy shouted before he disappeared in a splash and came up shaking the sparkling drops from his hair. "Free at last, free at last!" he crowed, slapping the water with his open hands. A dragonfly almost settled on his nose, but he swatted it away.

Rain gave me a look as if to say, You see what I have to put up with. I tried to hold her gaze, tried to get inside it and find out if there was any part just for me. She smiled quickly and then looked away.

The trees above the stream were filled with new green leaves and the sound of stirring among the branches—a squirrel leaping from one branch to the other, two mockingbirds balanced, swaying, with their tails up in the air.

"What're you thinking, Lizard?" Rain was floating on her stomach in shallow water and walking on the bottom with her hands, her legs straight out behind her.

"I had a friend who loved to swim."

"You'll have to bring him here. Sammy, you ought to show Lizard our cave."

"Shoot, it's probably just like the one he crawled out of."

"Lord," Rain said, "what am I going to do with you? You've got no manners at all." She walked with her hands to where Sammy was floating on his back, then got up on her knees, planted her hands firmly on his stomach, and tried to push him under. Her boobs were light on top and darker underneath. Sammy grabbed her wrists, and they struggled. She flipped like a fish. Then she stood and tried to get away from him, the water pushing out in front of her like a wake. The hair between her legs held the light in beads.

"No, Sammy. Stop! Don't, Sammy!" she shrieked. He caught her from behind and lifted her at the waist like he was going to throw her back into the stream. But instead, he let her slowly back down, turning her his way, and folded his long arms around her. She closed her eyes, linked her fingers behind his back, and nestled her head under his chin. That was some picture they made—the two of them black and dripping with sunlight in the middle of the stream while the dragonflies hovered in midair and the mockingbirds stretched their wings among the new green leaves.

"What are you looking at?" Sammy said to me.

"Damn you, Sammy." Rain beat her fists against him. "Be good to our guest, or I swear I'll take up and leave."

"Yeah?" he said, pushing her away.

"Yes, and then who'd do your cooking and sew up your raggedy old jeans and remember to pick your hat up out of the rain so it wouldn't shrink? God, you're a mess. If Mama only knew how you'd turned out to be—"

He clambered onto the bank. "What Mama had better have done was take care of her own self. You know what I mean. Instead of taking up with that one-eyed freak—"

"Shut up your talking about Mama," Rain said. She was standing on the bank opposite him now, her hands high on her hips.

Sammy snatched up his jeans and took off through the trees.

Rain stood there watching him, then stamped her feet. "Durn that boy. He drives me crazy." She paced the bank. "Why do I have to be fifteen? Why isn't it just the opposite, and then he'd have to take care of me. You got brothers or sisters?"

I shook my head.

"That's good. Don't ever feel like you missed out on anything." She sat, dangling her feet in the stream.

I waded over and straddled a log. "How long's it been since your mama died?" I asked.

"How'd you know that?"

"The way you and Sammy were talking."

Rain shielded her eyes from the sun. "We lost her two years ago last spring. She was taken in a flash flood when the stream jumped its banks. We never found her. Maybe she was carried to the sea."

"My daddy died before I was born," I said.

"What's your mama like?"

"I never did have one. Miss Cooley raised me. She worked at the L&N Café."

"I didn't think you could do that—not have a mama," Rain said.

"Do you have a daddy?"

"No," Rain said.

"Well, see, that's not supposed to be possible either."

Rain threw a rock into the stream. The ripples were like gold rings. "I know. Mama used to say that some things were not meant to be understood, just believed."

Suddenly she cocked her head. "Listen. Hear that?"

"What?"

"That bird."

Upstream buffalo gnats rose off the surface in small black clouds. I couldn't hear anything but the water over rocks.

"He's saying, 'Drink your tea,' " Rain said.

Then I did hear it, a long way away. Without a word Rain and I started walking along the bank of the stream, following that bird as if he might lead us to the place where the light began.

Instead, after a while, we came to the cave.

"Sammy thinks these are Indian markings," Rain said, running her hand over a star-shaped design on the rock face. "I think it's just a pattern in the rock itself. What do you think?"

The rock was cold and gray and flecked with pale lichen. "I don't know," I said. "But this does look like a place where Indians might camp."

The stream had narrowed and disappeared under a wide shelf of rock. The overhang had been high enough for us to walk right in for twenty yards or so. We didn't even have to stoop over much. After that the ceiling started to close in and it got dark. At the back the passage became a crawl space, but you could tell it opened into a larger room after that, because there was a steady stream of cold air and the sound of water dripping.

"Sammy's got a carbide lamp that he wears on a strap on his head," Rain says. "We got a flashlight, too, but I'm scared to go in. Two springs ago the crawl space got blocked with mud and rocks. Sammy thinks somebody did it on purpose. So ever since he's been trying to dig his way back in."

"Why?"

"I don't know," she said. "It's like something just gets hold of him."

The silence underneath the rock overhang was eerie. "I'm kind of cold," Rain said. "You want to go back?"

I nodded. I was cold, too, and the chill didn't leave

until we were back at the pump house, where Sammy waited for us with a sullen look on his face.

"Come on, Sammy," Rain said. "Let's drink from the silver bowl and tell stories."

"Where are your clothes?" he asked, arms folded.

"They're by the stream. I'll get them later. Come on. There are still huckleberries to eat." Rain reached for the honey and brown sugar while Sammy removed a few books from the topmost shelf. Behind them was a bright silver bowl, its edges outlined with what looked like branches and berries and leaves.

"I bet you think I stole this, don't you?" Sammy asked, but I hadn't said anything.

Rain brought the berries, and we sat in a triangle on the floor. Then Sammy poured something from a pitcher into the silver bowl.

"What's that?" I asked.

"It's nothing," Rain said. "Just water. But something happens to it in the bowl. You tell him, Sammy."

"I wouldn't waste my breath."

"You mean the water becomes something else?" I asked.

"No. It becomes itself," Rain said.

"What do you mean?"

Rain closed her eyes and spoke as though she were reading words from the inside of her lids: "We believe that when we drink from the silver bowl, the water becomes like it was before we were here, before anybody was here, before there was an orchard or even an earth. In the bowl the water becomes as pure as it was the moment it was first made, before it had touched anything except the imagination of the one who first imagined it."

"And let me tell you, *that* is pure," Sammy added.

"You really believe that?" I said.

Rain opened her eyes. "We know it," she said.

"Our great-great-grandfather told us about it," Sammy said. "In a dream."

"You had the same dream?" I asked.

"We used to," Rain answered simply. "Well, go ahead, drink."

I took the bowl and looked into it. It just looked like water to me. I took a sip. "I don't taste anything," I said.

Rain smiled.

"That's the whole point," Sammy said. "It's a very special bowl, you understand?"

I nodded, but of course I didn't.

"This bowl," Sammy continued, "was a princess's ransom. My great-great-grandfather's niece." He paused, as if waiting for me to disagree. "She was kidnapped by the Cherokee because of her high cheekbones and her way with speech. They thought she'd make a good bride for their new chief. Stop looking like you don't believe me."

"I swear I do," I said.

Sammy drank from the bowl and passed it to Rain. She did the same and passed it back to me.

"Narrow Meadow, my great-great-grandfather, swore revenge," Sammy said. "But the Cherokee chief sent a message that Narrow Meadow could have his niece if the Creeks brought a gift to the Cherokees. The catch was that it had to be a special gift, a particular gift, a silver bowl that the Cherokee chief had seen in a museum in Boston, on a visit with a French general." Sammy swallowed deeply from the bowl. "Where was I?"

"The bowl's in Boston," Rain said, taking the bowl once again.

"The bowl's in Boston. Don't you see? Chief Narrow

Meadow was the smartest of the Creeks, but he'd never heard of Boston. Still, he said sure, we'll have that bowl in no time, give it to you as a sign of respect, and take back our niece. Nobody wants a war anyway, do they?"

The bowl was still in Boston, I thought, passing it to Rain. The sunlight came through the window in two solid gold bars.

"Then do you know what he did?" Sammy asked. "To find out where Boston was, Narrow Meadow left his tribe and disguised himself as a deaf slave." It was as though these weren't Sammy's own words, but something he'd memorized. "He was sold to a tobacco warehouse in Carolina, then hopscotched from one farm to the next up the Rappahannock to Maryland, where he escaped and finally made it to Boston in the back of a potato farmer's wagon. After that it was easy. He stole the silver bowl from the Boston Museum, put on his buckskins again, and disappeared into the woods."

"Hurry, Sammy," Rain said. "I want to tell him about our great-great-grandmother."

"I'll tell it the way I want to," Sammy said. "When he got back here, he told the craftsmen in the tribe to make a copy of the bowl out of thin Navaho lead that he had bartered two hundred muskrat skins for. The copy was perfect right down to the smith's mark on the bottom. And that was the bowl he took to the Cherokee chief. The Cherokees couldn't believe he'd actually found the bowl and stolen it. But they accepted the bowl, the copy that is, and returned Narrow Meadow's niece."

"Why'd he go to all that trouble?" I asked.

Sammy swished the water in his mouth before he swallowed. "Revenge," he slowly said. "Narrow Meadow told the local agents from the Bureau of Indian Affairs that

the Cherokee chief had stolen a valuable bowl from the
Boston Museum. The chief was arrested, sent off to Boston, and hanged. Although there hadn't been a war between the Cherokees and the Creeks, the Cherokee chief
was dead, and my great-great-grandfather not only had
the silver bowl, but he also had his niece.''

We sat cross-legged in silence until Rain finally looked
at me and said, ''All right, now this is the story of our
great-great-grandmother, who was a slave on a farm in
Maryland, on the banks of the Rappahannock. She slept
with a man who spoke a language she couldn't understand. But with his hands he told her a story about a
bright bowl far away and a woman relative in trouble. A
month later he escaped. She had a daughter by this
stranger, and when she was finally freed, she brought her
daughter to this part of Louisiana to live. They share-
cropped on land near the road west and bartered with
the Creeks, who were walking to Oklahoma and selling
their valuables cheap. A young Creek woman had a bowl
to sell. With her hands she told a confusing tale about an
uncle of hers, a brave and noble chief, who had won her
from the Cherokees by pretending to be a slave. In an
instant our great-great-grandmother knew the stories
were the same. She bought the bowl with food and cloth
and gave her cabin as a permanent resting place for the
Creeks. Then she passed the bowl along to her daughter,
who she now knew to be the daughter of a chief. That
daughter was our great-grandmother, half slave and half
Creek. She told our mother the story of the silver bowl
and left it to her when she died, and our mother told us
the story and now we're telling it to you.''

I felt my scalp tingle. ''So you really are Creek!''

''What the hell have I been telling you all this time,''

Sammy said. "You honkies never believe anything we say."

"Sammy, be kind," Rain said. "Remember how Mama would want us to be."

"This is the last time I'm warning you, Rain. Don't Mama me. You should've Mama'd Mama. That's what you should have done. Told her to stay away from one-eyed preachers with hollow legs. Then we wouldn't be in the fix we're in today." Sammy stood and put the bowl back on the shelf.

"Don't talk about Mama that way. I'll tell Aunt Eunice!" Rain turned to me. "Mama's sister Eunice lives in Detroit. She's coming back to get us when she saves enough money."

"In the meantime—" Sammy said, standing over her.

"In the meantime we stay put right here."

"And every two weeks or so *he* comes here, that half-blind snake."

"He brings us food," Rain said.

"And he eats twice what he brings."

"He gives us letters from Aunt Eunice."

"In which she tells us to stay away from him."

"He—"

"What else does he do, Rain? Tell Lizard what else he does while I'm away."

Rain stood up. "What do you care? You're in the cave digging all day. I don't know where you think you're digging."

"I'm digging a way out of here, to China or Mississippi, I don't care which. In the meantime, what are you doing, Rain?"

She walked to the window, put her hands on the pane,

and stared out of it as though she were watching the way the sunlight played upon the stream.

"Life can't always be gay," she said.

"That's just what Mama used to say," Sammy hissed, and he sat so hard, the card table shook. The sunlight fell in bars across his face.

I followed Rain out onto the steps of the pump house. A shadow had fallen across the stream. I sat beside her on the topmost step. Her legs were smooth and dark. Mine were pale and skinny and bowed below the knee.

"That preacher Sammy was talking about," she said. "He's not really a preacher. He just claims to be. He was Mama's boyfriend a long time ago, and he says he's got the papers to show that we belong to him. Even though he lives in town, he's what they call a guardian. That means he can come out here drunk every so often, beat Sammy, and have his way with me."

"You've got to get away from here."

"We don't have any money. Besides, he's got those papers. He can do anything he wants. Sammy tried to run away one time, but the deputies brought him back. I'm afraid Sammy's going to kill him if he ever gets the chance."

"Well, he better not come around while I'm here."

Rain smiled.

"I'm serious," I said.

"Just come back sometime," Rain said. "Sammy and I have never really had a friend."

The sunlight came low through the trees. Already a pale moon had appeared. We waited on the steps until the insects struck up, and I realized how late I was going to be getting back to the spot where the actors and I had camped.

"I had a good time today," I said.

"Me too," Rain said. "I felt like Mama was still alive."

Without thinking I put my arm around her. I'd never been so close to a girl before, and it felt like there were feathers in my stomach.

For a long time I held her like that, and then I told her I'd be back. She handed me the rabbit traps in a gunnysack. It was heavier than it should have been. "We ate your rabbits." She smiled.

"I know. Now, remember, I'll be back."

I found my clothes on the bank. They were cold and damp. I dressed, and before I got out of sight, I turned to take one more look at the pump house. The moon was like broken glass on the stream.

6

ON MY WAY back through the orchards and woods, I got lost. Instead of taking time to get my bearings, to stake out a center and search in widening circles until I came back to the stream, I panicked. With the moon rising above the trees I took off in what I thought was the right direction, only to run into a barbed-wire fence that I hadn't seen before and the remains of an abandoned fire tower. I tried to backtrack toward the pump house, but nothing looked familiar, so I went at a right angle into the dark pines. Luck was with me. I found the stream. But after following it for thirty minutes I came to a highway bridge that I knew I hadn't seen before, so I had to turn back around. By this time the moon was almost directly overhead. It was more than half full, but I still couldn't see well enough to tell where I might be. The gunnysack was getting heavier by the minute. I stopped in my tracks. I listened. I waited for some kind of sign, and when nothing came to me I took off again through the

woods, following nothing more than a compass I sometimes have in my head. In this way I finally came to the
spot where we'd pulled off the road. The truck was nowhere to be seen. I didn't lose hope, because I'd learned
that things never work out the way you plan. Maybe this
wasn't the same spot after all. Maybe the actors were
waiting a little farther down the road. But then I found
what was left of our campfire. The coals had been scat-
tered and the ground picked clean. There weren't any
cans or Hershey-bar wrappers or footprints. The road
was empty as far as I could see. The sky seemed empty,
too, and cold. Even the stars were slung out into space
like somebody didn't want us to know he had camped
there.

Suddenly I saw headlights in the trees. They appeared
to be coming slow. If it was the truck, I'd have time to flag
it down, but if it wasn't the truck and it was going that
slow, I wasn't sure I wanted to be seen. So I slipped
behind a tree.

At the place where Callahan had pulled off the road,
the headlights stopped. Somebody shone a light on the
tracks the truck's tires had made, then flashed the light
toward the orchard. It was a sheriff's car. Three men got
out. Each of them had a flashlight, and they were searching the ground between the road and the orchard. Even
though the moon was bright, I couldn't be sure that the
two in uniform were the deputies who had stopped us
the day before. But I thought I recognized those cauliflower ears. The third man didn't wear a uniform. He was
black and taller than the other two, and he had a head so
huge, it drooped from his shoulders like it was too heavy
to carry upright.

"If they did stay here, we'll find some sign of them!" shouted the deputy with the cauliflower ears.

"Don't be so sure, Roger," the other deputy said. "If they could make us think a boy was a dog, I'd say they could do most anything."

"Don't include me in that 'us' of yours," said the deputy with cauliflower ears. "I wasn't suckered in for a minute."

"Shoot, Roger, don't feed me that. You were the one that asked about the breed."

"That's what I mean. I knew something was screwy from the start."

"Well, if that's so, how come on the way back, all you talked about was hiring that thing to stud your spitz?"

"It was because of the unusual nature of the animal, that's why. I'd never seen a dog like that and had my suspicions from the start. You didn't even look twice. Wouldn't know a Doberman from a doormat, and here you're complaining about me!"

The black man shone his flashlight directly into the deputy's face. "Will you two stop wasting my time? I'm going to find that runaway from the retard school whether you want to help or not."

"I want to find him too," Roger shouted. "Nobody makes a fool of me like that."

"They don't have to," the other deputy said. "You were born that way."

"For Christ's sake, shut up!" the black man yelled. "Now, somebody help me find the son of a bitch who stole my property."

"Don't you worry, Reverend. We'll get him." The deputy trotted away, and the black man played his flashlight toward my tree. I made myself small and wondered what he meant by his property. They were moving in wide circles now, spaced evenly apart. There wasn't a sound except the swish of weeds against the searchers' legs. The black man was getting so close, I could smell the hard, sweet whiskey that came off him like a cloud. For a minute the flashlight seemed to disappear, so I took a chance and stuck my head around the tree. The black man was crouched in a circle of dirt, his flashlight pointing straight down at a cigar butt that Callahan had forgotten to pick up. The black man grunted, and the flashlight casually swung up, catching his face from underneath. Where his left eye should have been, there was nothing, no eyeball, no patch, just an empty socket that glowed pink where the light touched the rim.

"You can stop searching!" he hollered over his shoulder. "They camped here, all right." He stood up, and the deputies waded through the weeds to him, their handcuffs jangling against their belts. "The truck's long gone, but I've got a hunch the retard is still in these woods. I can smell the little shithead. Tomorrow you'll need to bring the dogs. We'll start at the road and work our way in. The dogs'll see to it that he coughs up my silver bowl."

"You don't think Sammy could have hid it? He's a bad one," said the deputy with the cauliflower ears.

"If he had, that whipping would have got it out of him. His sister would have confessed just to spare him. Look, my belt buckle's twisted out of shape."

The deputies whistled and shook their heads. "You're tough on them. You know, that sister of his ain't bad looking. You need somebody to teach her how to behave?"

"I can take care of my own," the preacher said.

"Boy, I'd sure like to have a chance at her," said the deputy with cauliflower ears. "I spied her swimming naked in that stream while I was hunting deer. I almost stopped to say hello, but shoot, you never know what you might catch from one of them."

"One of who?" The preacher glowered.

"Didn't mean a thing by it, Reverend. Just talking about kids, living out in the woods like that."

"Well, there's nothing more to do here tonight. We'll bring the dogs out at sunrise. Let's get back to town. Didn't I promise I'd set you boys up to a drink?"

"I'm mighty glad you remembered that, Reverend," said one of the deputies as they walked back toward the highway. They climbed into the sheriff's car, the doors slammed, the engine jolted into gear, and the last I saw of the preacher was a single red taillight glowing down the road. The other one was burned out.

Deep in the orchard a dog howled. Something touched me on the shoulder. I yelled, scraping my ear against the tree.

"It's just me," a voice said. When I turned around, the moonlight fell full on Callahan's foxlike face. "Where have you been all day?" he said. I didn't answer, but just threw my arms around his neck so that we both fell back into the weeds.

"Whoa, Lizard, take it easy. They didn't scare you that much, did they? Why, those three wouldn't make proper villains in the plays we put on. The kids in grade school would laugh them off the stage. Come on. Sallie's waiting for us at the bridge."

I scrambled off Callahan and found the gunnysack with the traps. "We've got to come back here tomorrow," I said.

"I'm afraid that'll have to wait. We've got to get to Birmingham. Besides, it's too hot for us around here. What happened to you today? We were worried to death."

I was following Callahan through the moonlight. The pump house seemed like a dream. "I met some kids where we set out the traps."

"That was the first place I looked." He sounded like he didn't believe me. "What was that black guy saying about a silver bowl?"

"I know what he was talking about. But I didn't steal it."

Callahan stopped and turned toward me. "I didn't say you did. Are you feeling all right, Lizard?" We stared at each other and I nodded my head. Then Callahan took off again, faster now, snapping the branches back in my face. I was having to run to keep up.

"Where are we now?" I asked, so I'd know how to get back when I could.

"Twelve miles east of Newllano," Callahan said. "We clocked it on the way to town."

Twelve miles east of Newllano, I repeated over and over to myself. For all I could think about was Rain.

7

I'D NEVER known how flat Louisiana was until we crossed the Mississippi River at Vicksburg and I looked back. As far as I could see, the land lay brown and green, wavy in the early-morning heat, but the line where it touched the sky was like the slit a razor had made. The other bank of the river was overgrown and steep. The first person I saw in Mississippi was a woman whose boobs were coming out of her dress. She stood in front of a Burger King, waving at somebody on a Greyhound bus. I felt like I'd traveled a thousand miles. It was the first time I'd ever been in another state. I just couldn't believe that Mississippi had really been there all my life.

When we passed a dead armadillo at an intersection, Callahan popped another beer and said, "Guess how he got here from Louisiana."

"How do you know he came from Louisiana?"

Callahan flicked his cigar ash. "All armadillos are from Louisiana, and before that Texas, and before that Mexico. They've been heading north and east for centuries now, on their way to the Atlantic Ocean, and one day they'll be there. The hard thing so far has been crossing the Mississippi River. They can't swim."

"So how'd they do it?" Sallie asked.

"They walked across the bottom."

"Come on."

"That's right. They sink to the bottom and walk across holding their breath."

"You've got this thing about armadillos, don't you?" Sallie said.

"Is he telling the truth?" I asked Sallie.

"Don't ask me."

I looked at Callahan. He had polished off the beer.

"Speaking of the truth," he said, the cigar clenched between his teeth, "run that by me again about that black girl and her brother living in a pump house by a stream." He grinned.

"Cal," Sallie said, "don't start that up again."

"We were just having a discussion, weren't we, Lizard? About the nature of fiction and truth."

"I don't know what that means," I said. We were barreling through the suburbs of Vicksburg, past shopping malls with yellow banners flying on their roofs, school buses, churches with brick steeples, Eckerd's discount drugs. Callahan's foot was so heavy on the gas, the truck rocked back and forth like it might tear loose from itself. Mac started barking in the back.

"We're all of us tired," Sallie said. "All we need is a good night's sleep."

The place we stopped at was a glass-front Ramada Inn. The lobby had drapes three stories high, spiral staircases with orange carpet, and a chandelier that looked like glass milk cartons strung together with gold rope. Standing in the parking lot while Callahan got the key, I could hear the clean song of a red-winged blackbird, though I hadn't seen him yet. Behind the motel was a marsh with sawgrass and cottonwood trees. He'd probably be sitting on a fence post back there.

Our room smelled like insect repellant and Sani-Flush. It had a big color TV, two beds, and a strip of paper around the toilet seat. Callahan and Sallie wanted to take a nap, but I wasn't a bit sleepy. All I wanted to do was hit the swimming pool. Sallie cut off the legs of my jeans, saying we'd get another pair in Birmingham anyway. Then she hung a DO NOT DISTURB sign on the door. "Come on, Mac," I said. He crawled under one of the beds, so I went by myself, following the arrows past the ice machine to the pool.

I'd never been swimming in a concrete pool. There had been one at the De Ridder Community Center, but it closed because of integration and never opened up again. When I stood on the edge of that Ramada Inn pool, I felt like I was from another time. The water was blue and so clear that the light on the bottom came together and broke apart like a living jigsaw puzzle. I jumped in. The water didn't feel soft and slick, like Alligator Lake. It was cold. Goose bumps broke out all over me, so I started swimming from one end to the other to get warm quick. Then I saw I wasn't alone.

Two girls were suspended under the diving board, holding to it and facing one another. I stopped in the middle of the pool and dog-paddled, not wanting to get too close to them. Nobody else was around except for a boy sitting in one of the chairs at the edge. He had red hair and wore a long-sleeve shirt.

I climbed out of the pool and lay on the hot concrete so the sun could dry me off. Hearing the girls giggling and splashing, I looked up.

"Harrison!" one of them cried. She had blond hair and sunburned shoulders. "Bobbie's got a crush on your friend over there." The boy with red hair leaned back in his chair and pretended to be watching a cloud.

"Shut up, Ginger," the other girl said. "He can hear you."

The girls whispered to each other, and Ginger said, "How should I know? Why don't you ask him yourself?" But then she looked in my direction. "Hey, boy!" she yelled. "My friend Bobbie wants to know what happened to your face." I didn't say anything. "She wants to know if you were in an accident or something."

Bobbie kicked at Ginger above water. "Stop it!" Ginger squealed. "You'll get my hair wet!"

"I'm going in," Bobbie announced, and she swung up onto the edge of the pool. Her legs were tanned and muscular, like she'd lived in the water all her life.

"What's the matter?" Ginger asked. "You got to get ready for your big date? There ain't no hurry. He's sitting right here by the pool."

Bobbie twirled her towel into a rat's tail and flicked it at Ginger from the pool's edge. "Stop it!" Ginger said. Then she let go of the diving board and sank straight down, her hair unloosening like a cloud. In a second she reappeared at the edge closest to the boy with red hair. She folded her arms on the concrete and let her legs dangle behind her. "Tell me the truth, Harrison," she said. "Are you listening to me? Who do you like best, Bobbie or me?"

Harrison squinted at her like he'd sat on something sharp.

"Why don't you just leave me alone?" he said.

"Oh, I get it," she said, pushing off from the edge and back-paddling. "You mean you just don't like girls at all!" She climbed out of the water as far from Harrison as she could get, as though he had something she might catch. "I knew there was something weird about you," she said. She walked away squeezing her hair, her bathing suit dripping on the concrete.

Harrison looked over at me and shook his head like there was nothing more you could say about girls. "You play gin rummy?" he asked.

"No," I said. "What's that?"

"It's a card game. You like cards, don't you?"

"I've never played cards."

He settled back in his chair but then sat up again quick. "Want a Coke?"

"Sure, but I don't have any money."

"I got some. Don't worry." And he disappeared into the hallway where the drink and ice machines were. When he came back with the Cokes, he smiled, wrinkling his nose.

"Thanks," I said. "I'll pay you back."

"That's okay. It's my dad's money. Is your dad here?"

That was a funny question to ask right off, I thought. "No, I'm on business."

"Business? How old are you?"

"Sixteen," I lied. "I'm small for my age. I'm an actor."

Harrison's eyes widened. He looked in the direction where the girls had disappeared, as if he'd like to tell them that and see what they had to say then. "Have I ever seen you on TV?"

"I doubt it," I said.

"Oh." I think he knew then I was pulling his leg. Harrison didn't look like he belonged by the pool. He was too dressed up. He had on brown pants without belt loops and a brown-and-white long-sleeve polo shirt. His socks were brown, too, and his tennis shoes were so new, they didn't even have scuff marks. It made me hot to look at him.

"You been swimming yet?" I asked.

"I don't know how. Besides, I don't like girls to see me without a shirt on. I'm kinda fat."

"I wouldn't much care what those girls thought."

"Oh, I don't. They're nothing to me. Just met them yesterday when we pulled in. My dad and me. That's our car over there." He pointed to a bottle-green Buick convertible with Texas tags. I couldn't put my finger on it, but he reminded me of Mike.

"That's some car," I said.

"Yeah. It's got power windows and turbo-glide. Where's your car?"

"That truck there."

"Wow. Is it Army surplus?"

"I don't know."

"That's what I'll ask Dad to get next. I never knew anybody with a truck like that. What's your dad look like?"

"Look like?"

"Uh-oh," Harrison said. I turned to see Ginger and Bobbie in matching red shorts and white blouses. They were sipping Cokes with straws under an umbrella.

"What'll we do now?" he said. Already I could hear the

girls' thin laughter carried by the wind. And above it the sound of that red-winged blackbird, trilling cool and secretly from the cattails in the marsh.

"You ever seen a muskrat?" I asked.

"What's that?"

"You'll see. We might even catch a rabbit. I got some traps in the truck."

"Where would we catch them?"

"Down there by the water and the weeds."

"I don't know." Harrison frowned. "I'm not supposed to leave the motel. There are probably snakes down there."

"I hope so. Come on." Right then it occurred to me that Harrison probably hadn't done a lot of things. Maybe he'd driven across the country in a bottle-green Buick with Texas tags, but if he didn't know what a muskrat was, what kind of life was that? Right now the girls were looking at him and whispering. That seemed to do the trick. "Let's hurry," he said. "I got to get back before my dad finds out I'm gone."

The minute we got to the water, I knew I hadn't made a mistake. It was slimy and broken by stumps and logs, a perfect place for muskrats and snakes. Harrison saw a turtle sunning, and it nearly scared him out of his wits. He fell into a drainage ditch up to his knees. It startled him, but his face suddenly broke into a grin. Those tennis shoes would never be the same. We found two baby musk turtles by dredging the bottom with an old Crisco can. And an orange newt no longer than my thumb. Then, rounding a bend, we surprised a blue heron fishing for minnows. It took off with its wings creaking, and Harrison said that was the prettiest bird he'd ever seen.

As I watched Harrison struggle through the weeds with his pants legs dripping from the cuffs, I knew I needed a friend like him, but I also knew that after the next day I'd never see him again.

I swung the gunnysack with the traps onto the bank. "I'm tired of dragging this around," I said. "Let's go ahead and set them up." When I reached into the sack, I felt something that shouldn't have been there. It was smooth and round, and I think I knew what it was even before I brought it all the way up—Rain and Sammy's silver bowl.

"Where'd you get that?" Harrison asked. I was almost as surprised as he was. I held the bowl at arm's length and turned it, watching the sunlight jump from one bunch of silver leaves and fruit to the next. It felt like I was holding Rain's smile in my hands.

"There's something inside," Harrison said.

I looked. In the bowl was a note written on part of a grocery sack. *Dear Lizard,* it said. *Please sell this bowl when you get somewhere where you can mail the money to my Aunt Eunice Bertram, 901 Twelfth Street, Detroit, Michigan 48233. Maybe then she can come get us. Sammy will go crazy when he sees it's gone. But if we don't do something now, the preacher will take it anyway. He was eyeing it the last time he was here. I know you will do me this favor, and I can't wait to see you again. Hurry back to us, Lizard, as soon as you can.* And on the back, it said, *Please don't tell a soul about this. Rain.*

"What's it say?" Harrison asked, trying to peek over my shoulder.

"It's nothing," I said, folding up the note and stuffing it into the pocket of my cutoffs.

"Nothing? Come on, Lizard, where'd you get this thing?"

"It belongs to a girl I met and her brother." Then I caught myself, for Rain had said not to tell a soul.

"Is she your girlfriend?"

I didn't say anything.

"Come on, Lizard. Why can't you tell me about her?"

I thought about it a minute and then decided I could tell him a little, as long as I didn't talk about trying to sell the silver bowl and Rain's Aunt Eunice. So I told him about the day in the peach orchard when I came upon the pump house while looking for these very same traps. I tried to draw a picture for Harrison of what it was like, how mean Sammy seemed at first, the food we ate, the sunlight on the stream.

"You mean you didn't wear bathing suits?" he asked, his mouth a perfect circle in the middle of his freckled face. "What'd the girl look like? What's her name?"

"Rain," I said.

"She and her brother are in trouble, aren't they?" he asked.

"How'd you know that?"

"I can tell. The way you're acting. Don't they have a mom and dad?"

"Their mama's dead. I don't know about their daddy. A preacher is their guardian."

"That's good," Harrison said, and he seemed grateful for all the facts.

"That depends on how you look at it," I said. "He doesn't treat them right. There's no telling what he does to Rain. And he beats her brother bad."

"Oh," Harrison said. A cloud seemed to pass over his face.

"Well, we better get back," I said, putting the bowl back in the gunnysack with the traps. There was no use setting them out. We trudged through the weeds, leaving the still, green water behind us. The mosquitoes were getting bad. And the air was hot and heavy. Every step we took made a sucking sound because of the mud.

We were almost to the motel before Harrison spoke again. "My mom and dad are divorced," he said. "She's in Georgia. That's where I go to school. But I'm going to spend the summer in Texas with my dad." He stopped, sucking his cheek, like he was trying to think what to say next. "Rain and her brother. What's his name?"

"Sammy," I said.

He nodded. "That preacher who's their guardian and beats them."

"What about him?"

"My dad's like that."

I started to say something, but that blackbird had struck up again, and his song was so painful, I didn't have anything else to add.

The door to the room was opened a crack, but the chain was latched on the other side. It sounded like Callahan and Sallie were arguing. Mac whined when their voices rose too high.

"It interferes with your work, your acting," Sallie was saying.

"How can it interfere with something that doesn't exist? This is the first real acting job I've had in two years."

"That's what I mean," she said.

"What do you mean that's what you mean? Are you saying I haven't been trying to get work?"

"No. I know you have, in your own way."

"Wait a minute. You think I get a kick out of unloading plumbing supplies?"

"I said you've been trying. You've just let some good opportunities get away."

"Why are you riding me like this?" he said. "You know what acting's like. I can't help it if it's hard to break in."

"You're thirty, Cal. It's not breaking in anymore."

"The hell it isn't. I believe in my abilities."

"I do too. I'm not saying that."

"Well, what are you saying?"

"You've got to do something about your drinking."

"Now, wait a minute."

"That's just it, Cal. I have been waiting. I've been waiting for something to happen."

"To who? To me?"

"I think you're a great actor, Cal. I really do."

"But what?"

"Something's got to happen soon."

"Why doesn't something have to happen to you?"

"I can do other things," she said.

Mac smelled me at the door and stuck his nose through the opening, licking and snorting. I walked away and sat under an umbrella by the pool while the sun went down like a thin, hot wafer. When I went back to the room, the door was unlocked. Callahan and Sallie were asleep on the bedspread, one of his arms thrown around her, and their clothes were rumpled and stuck to their backs like another set of skin.

The next morning I saw Harrison coming out of the restaurant with a big red-haired man in a cowboy hat. "Hey, Lizard!" he shouted. "Come here and meet my dad!"

"Hi there, little 'un," the man said. "Harrison told me what you-all did yesterday. And I'm mighty thankful there's boys like you who will play with a kid even though he's fat." Now, that's a weird sense of humor, I thought to myself, but Harrison didn't seem to mind.

He pulled me over to the side. "Write and tell me what happened to Rain," he said. "Here's my address. Okay?"

His father was hemmed in by two waitresses who were carrying on about his snakeskin boots.

"Are you all right?" I asked Harrison, for his eyes were unnaturally bright.

"Sure!" he said in a voice that was louder than necessary, and a waitress rushed over with the cowboy hat he'd left at their table.

"Don't they look the pair!" she said, and Harrison's father reached over to straighten the hat. It was a huge hand, red and hard, with a gold ring set with a square stone.

"Let's hit the trail, little guy," he said, and the waitresses laughed, and Harrison laughed along with them, the loudest of all.

Callahan and Sallie had been checking out in the motel lobby. I came up to them just as the clerk was saying, "I'm sorry, but we won't be able to honor this credit card."

"What seems to be the problem?" Callahan asked in his Simonetti voice.

"I think you probably know," the clerk said slowly. "But if you'd like to talk to the manager, he's in his office now."

Callahan winked at Sallie. "There's probably something wrong with the computer. You and Lizard go on to the truck. And make sure we've got some fresh water for Mac."

"Let's go, Lizard," Sallie said. She had taken a shower and smelled like roses.

We hadn't been in the truck more than a minute or so when Callahan opened the door and jumped in. "All set?" he said.

"That didn't take long," Sallie answered.

"Just a screwup in the computer." He gunned the engine and settled it into reverse. I watched to be sure he cleared the car next to him. Then he shoved it into first, and we were off.

"Wait a minute, Cal. I forgot my bathing suit," Sallie said.

"They can mail it to us."

"Why? Let's just stop. We're not even out of the parking lot."

"You can get a new one in Birmingham." The truck's exhaust belched blue and swirled around us. Callahan lurched into the traffic, and someone honked.

Sallie sat up straight in the seat. "Are you crazy? Now, turn around and let me run in and get my bathing suit."

"I'm sorry," he said. "I can't do that."

I was worried. This hadn't happened before. And sure enough, we coughed blue smoke all the way to Birmingham.

8

I COULDN'T wait to see what downtown Birmingham was like, but Callahan took us first to a neighborhood called Southside. He said he wanted to get a look at the theater before we checked in at our hotel. The street we drove down was wide and lined with crape myrtles, and sometimes, between the trees, I'd catch a glimpse of the tall buildings downtown, gray and solid, but kind of unreal in the wavy heat. The houses in this particular neighborhood were huge and back a ways from the street. Men wearing ponytails sat on the front steps smoking cigarettes, and around back it looked like there were compost heaps and volleyball nets and dog runs with morning glory vines all over the place. Garbage cans spilled out into the street.

We came to a traffic circle beneath a clock advertising a brand of milk. Facing the traffic circle was a pool hall called Little Bombers with rows of motorcycles parked out front. Next to it was a flower shop and a post office.

Across the street was a restaurant with a foreign-looking name.

"That's it," Callahan said.

"The Golden Temple Emporium?" Sallie asked.

"Yeah. The theater's on the second floor, around back. Waldo says the Golden Temple used to be a delicatessen and bakery. The entire top floor was its kitchen. Then some health food types bought the building. They didn't need all that space in the kitchen upstairs to make their bean sprout sandwiches, so they leased it to Waldo and he turned it into a theater." Callahan made a left at the next light, shoved the gearshift into low to take the hill, and pulled into a driveway at the back of the restaurant.

The sign to the left of the theater entrance looked freshly painted: SOUTHSIDE REPERTORY COMPANY. Yellow flowers lined the brick walk. In a courtyard off to the side was a birdbath, some newly planted ferns, and a couple of banana trees with Christmas tree lights strung up in them.

Callahan pounded the steering wheel. "All right!"

But Sallie said, "I'll stay out here. I think it's bad luck to see the inside of a theater before rehearsals begin."

Sallie was right. When we opened the door I nearly gagged on the stink. The lobby was nothing but a narrow hallway that opened onto a room where somebody was using a blowtorch to melt the linoleum off the floor. A woman with a hoe came along behind trying to scrape up the mess. The air was filled with smoke and dust. From each corner of the room came pounding and curses. Workmen had hoisted what looked like a furnace to the ceiling and were trying to secure it with chains. Others were knocking down walls with sledgehammers. In the center of the room a woman was standing on the top of a stepladder, smoking a cigarette while she painted an already black skylight black.

"Oh, my God," Callahan said. He stood by the ladder and slowly turned around in disbelief. "Waldo," he said, but nobody could have heard him above the din. "Waldo!" he shouted much louder.

"Hey, Waldo!" the woman on the stepladder said without taking her eyes off the window. She was squinting against the smoke. "You got a visitor," she said.

The pounding in one corner of the room stopped. A bare-legged man in a raincoat and boots, his hair at all angles like a fright wig, appeared out of the smoke. His face was blackened with soot, and he was carrying a sledgehammer.

"Waldo?" Callahan said.

The man stared at Callahan for a full five seconds before he dropped the sledgehammer and swallowed him in a bear hug. "Maureen!" he yelled over his shoulder. "Look who's here."

The woman on the stepladder put down her brush. "Thank God. You've got to do something with Waldo. He's driving me crazy."

Waldo held Callahan at arm's length. "I hope you've got your lines."

"Look . . ." Callahan began.

"So what do you think?" Waldo asked, spreading his arms wide to take in the whole room.

"That's what I was about to say."

"You *like* it! I knew you would. I mean, it's not much to look at now, but the show doesn't open for—"

"Three weeks," Callahan said.

"Seventeen days, to be precise," Waldo said. "Actually

fourteen days of rehearsal, because Miranda's got to fly to Europe for her mother's wedding. It's her fourth husband, well, actually her third, since this is the second time around for them—"

"Waldo," Callahan said.

"Come on, come on. Let me take you on the tour. Watch out for the hot linoleum—" Suddenly he stopped and looked straight at me. "You brought a midget!" he said, clapping his hands.

"This is Lizard Sims, from Louisiana," Callahan said in a dispirited voice. "He's going to play Caliban."

Waldo's smile soured. "Caliban? But what about that Koswinski guy? The programs are already printed."

"Jerry had to cancel," said Callahan. "But think about the possibilities."

Waldo looked me over like I was a suit he was fixing to buy. I stared back at him with first one eye and then the other. He brushed the hair out of my face. "Cute idea," he finally said. "Real cute idea. Can he act?" Callahan didn't say anything. "Yeah, well, when has that ever stopped us, right?" Waldo continued. "Look at this, Maureen. It's not a midget. It's a kid." Then he turned back to me. "If I can get a decent performance out of somebody like Callahan, I can make a *star* out of you. Or I'm not Waldo Stakes."

He steered Callahan by the arm as they stepped over all kinds of wires and chunks of concrete. "Admittedly, we've still got some finishing touches to do on the house. But look, we've got a fabulous light booth here." He pulled at a heavy door that opened onto what looked like a walk-in refrigerator. "Remind me to get rid of those meat hooks," he said under his breath.

"Where's the dressing room?" Callahan asked.

"Funny you should ask. We're lucky, I mean really lucky, to have a beauty school next door. Mirrors, chairs with space-helmet hair dryers, the whole works. They use it during the day. We use it at night. I was just making an entrance to it." He had paused by a wall with an enormous ragged hole in it. Piles of plaster lay everywhere. Drawn in yellow chalk was the outline of a door. "Fire inspector said we'd have to have another exit anyway, so we broke through the ladies' room and I'm knocking out this door, gonna put up a Sheetrock tunnel—"

"Please," Callahan said. "I can't listen to this anymore."

"You nervous, Cal? Don't be nervous. I'm the director. Let *me* be nervous, okay?" His voice was rising. "But let's not forget, this is not the play. Right? This is only the physical space where it takes place. The real play is in the mind, the imagination."

Maureen had sidled up, puffing on her cigarette. "Yeah, we always make it by opening night," she said.

Waldo turned on her. "That's easy for you to say. You don't have to sweet-talk Miranda's orthodontist or wring Alabama accents out of the lords from Milan."

"I'm just trying to be optimistic," Maureen said.

"Optimism. God knows we need it. We hardly have a theater. We don't have a set. And please don't mention the rest of the season."

"What about the season?" Callahan asked.

"Later. Let's get something to eat." Waldo stuck his hands in the pockets of his raincoat. "Well, come on," he said, his eyes welling. "There won't be many more meals after this one."

* * *

"We can't do it," Waldo said when we had ordered cucumber sandwiches and herbal tea at the Golden Temple restaurant downstairs.

"Do what?" Callahan asked.

"The season."

"What do you mean?"

"Didn't you get my note?" Waldo asked, red-eyed and grim. He had changed into regular clothes and had washed his face.

Callahan and Sallie stared at one another. "That's a lousy line," Callahan said. "You should never ask people who have driven seven hundred miles to get here and slept on the ground and borrowed money for gas—you should never say to these people: 'Didn't you get my note?' "

"I know. I sympathize. Really. It's the grant. The one from the government to underwrite our season."

"What about it?"

"We didn't get it."

Callahan's face turned pale.

"So who needs the government?" Waldo continued. *"We* need the government. We can't do a season without the government. That's what was in the note."

The waitress brought our food. She wore a towel around her head and a white bathrobe. Her leather sandals made a creaking sound. "Eat wisely," she said, "and you will have perfect peace."

Callahan looked like he might want to hurt her. "I don't get it," he said. "You promised us six months of repertory at equity pay—*The Tempest, Uncle Vanya,* that Tom Stoppard piece, the *Texas Trilogy*—"

"We're doing *The Tempest.* For one night, anyway. After that it's up to the house—"

"For one—Waldo, please help me understand. I haven't gotten paid to act in two years." The color was coming back to Callahan's face. "You know what I do for a living? I unload plumbing-supply trucks, part time. I borrowed three hundred dollars to get here." His face was definitely red now. "From my aunt, Waldo. She's eighty-six. She's got rheumatoid arthritis and lives in public housing in Houston where they kill people for less than what you've done to me! You're telling me that there isn't any season at equity pay, there isn't anything except *The Tempest* and that that—"

"Might not run past opening night," Waldo said with appreciation, as though Callahan had gotten a difficult problem right.

Callahan coughed, beat his chest like he was choking, then got up from the table and staggered out of the restaurant.

"He'll get over it," Waldo said. "Callahan's always been too high strung and dramatic. He exaggerates everything."

I didn't know what was going on, but I had to take a leak. I asked the waitress in the turban where the bathroom was. She told me, bowed, and said, "Go in perfect peace."

The bathroom had music piped in. It sounded like pots and pans and kazoos. When I got back to the table, Callahan still wasn't there. I could see him through the glass door, sitting on the curb with his head in his hands. Waldo was eating his cucumber sandwich, and Sallie was calmly blowing across the surface of her tea.

"Are we going to do the play?" I asked her.

"At least for one night," she said. "Maybe more. It depends on the reviews and the number of reservations.

Things don't ever turn out the way they're supposed to."
She took a sip of tea and smiled. She'd been through
worse, her smile seemed to say. I loved her, the woman
who had played Jim Hawkins and could turn cartwheels
all over the place.

"I couldn't have stayed long anyway," I said. "I've got
to get back to Rain."

"Who?"

But Callahan had reentered the restaurant and was
trying hard to control himself. "What time are rehearsals?" he finally asked.

"That a boy," Waldo said. "Day after tomorrow, nine
o'clock sharp for the read-through. We'll be blocking the
first act that afternoon at three."

He stuck out his hand for Callahan to shake. "No hard
feelings?" he said.

"We *will* get paid for *The Tempest*?" Callahan replied.

"Of course. What kind of business do you think we're
running here?" Waldo asked.

They shook, and Waldo said, "I just hope to God
you've got your lines learned."

9

ON THE WAY to the hotel Callahan stopped for tooth-
paste and another six-pack of beer. He had drunk two
cans by the time we crossed a viaduct into the middle of
downtown. I'd never been in a city bigger than Lake
Charles. There were just too many things to take in all at
once—buildings that reflected each other like mirrors,
policemen on horses, black men with jackhammers,
women leaning against telephone poles in dresses slit up
to their waists. Some men wore suits and sunglasses.
They carried briefcases and looked hard and mean. I felt
most at home on the run-down avenues, where the windows were boarded and the winos looked just like the
ones in Louisiana, except they probably couldn't speak
French.

De Ridder had been a little town where you never saw
anybody you'd never seen before, unless they were
soldiers from Fort Polk or their families. Birmingham,
though, was like a revolving screen on which the faces

changed every turn it made. The only people I'd known more than a day were Sallie and Callahan, and really, who were they?

Had I changed? Now that I wasn't in Louisiana anymore, was I anywhere? To Walrus and Ricardo and the other boys at the state school, I was just gone. To Miss Cooley I was a name. To Rain and Sammy I must have seemed like a ghost, there for a minute in the peach orchard and then nowhere to be seen. I knew what this feeling was I was having, because I'd felt the same way at the state school. It was worse than homesickness, because at least with that, you know what you miss. But how can you miss yourself?

"That's home," Callahan said, squinting through the windshield at an old brick building with a sign saying REDMONT HOTEL. The bottom-floor window had a picture of a naked woman taking a bath in a glass of champagne.

And the lobby had carpet that was more like worn green felt on a pool table. The overhead fans barely stirred up the heat. When the yellow-skinned clerk saw me, he said, "There ain't no doctor on duty here."

Callahan looked at him straight and said, "What makes you think we need one?"

"Just trying to be helpful" was all the clerk said.

The elevators were out of order, so we walked to the last floor before you got to the roof, into a sour-smelling hallway and a room without curtains, but with a view of the setting sun, which was lined up straight with one of the avenues and glowed orange in a building across town.

"I can't stay here without curtains," Sallie said.

"I'll complain at the desk," answered Callahan.

"Does it have a bathroom?" I asked.

"Down the hall."

"When can we get Mac out of the truck?"

"I'll bring him up the fire escape later."

"Is there any ice?"

"Stop asking me questions." Callahan flopped into a chair. "Just give me some time to think. I could use a drink. How about you?"

"Maybe later," Sallie said. "I just want to wash my face and lie down."

"Lizard, how about you bringing Mac up?"

I walked back down to the parking lot and lifted the flap to let Mac jump out. He rolled on his back on the asphalt, and I could see the fleas crisscrossing his stomach. For the first time since we'd left Vicksburg, I thought about the silver bowl. I decided to wrap it in a blanket and take it back to the room, thinking that tomorrow, bright and early, I'd try to find a place to sell it, an antique shop or a jewelry store. Then I'd mail the money to Rain's aunt, like she'd asked me.

The fire escape was tricky, but Mac and I made it to the hallway of the last floor before the roof, and when I knocked at the door, Sallie let us in.

"It's a little hot for a blanket, isn't it?"

"I brought it for Mac," I said. "Where's Callahan?"

"Downstairs in the bar, I guess." She looked older than she ever had to me. Her hair had come loose from where it had been pinned in back, and there were circles under her eyes from too many nights without a good sleep. "You hungry?" she asked.

"No."

"Me either." She sat down on the bed. "Why don't you tell me about the silver bowl."

I felt a shiver go through me, like I'd stepped on a

crack. She must have run across it in the truck and just not said anything. "It's not mine," I said.

"I know. Cal told me about the preacher and the deputies who were at the orchard where we camped."

"It's not the preacher's either." I sat on the floor and started petting Mac. "I didn't steal it. I bet you think I did."

"I wouldn't care if you had," Sallie said. "You're not my boy. You don't belong to me. I'm just interested in the story behind it, that's all."

Down the avenue the sun had disappeared, and the sky was violet, with a single star. There wasn't any reason to keep anything from Sallie. I told her about Sammy and Rain, the preacher, the bowl, the light upon the stream. She watched that star through the window while I talked, watched as it was joined by another and then another. I stopped talking about the time the streetlights came on.

"I can't wait to meet Rain," she said.

"What does it mean when somebody says, 'He has his way with me'?" I asked, remembering Rain's exact words.

Sally thought for a minute. "It can mean that somebody is having things just the way he wants them, even if it hurts somebody else. Or if a woman says it about a man, it can mean that he's forcing her to have sex with him." She must have seen the change come over my face. "There's nothing you can do right now. Things will work out all right when Rain's aunt comes to get them, Lizard. I guess what you need to do is try to sell that bowl."

I took it from the blanket and gave it to her. She held it to the light. "Don't just take it to an antique store. The director of the museum here is a friend of Waldo's.

Maybe he can tell you what it's really worth. Do you want me to help you with it?"

I shook my head.

"Whatever you want to do," she said.

Then Sallie began reading the play to me. It was called *The Tempest,* by William Shakespeare. I could hardly understand a single word she said. But some of it I understood without even knowing the words. Maybe it was the way she read the parts, or the sound of the strange words themselves. It started with a shipwreck. All the passengers had to jump overboard and swim to an island. The island was nearly deserted. But there was a man who lived there named Prospero and his daughter Miranda. Prospero was some kind of magician or king. He had a slave named Caliban. Sallie said that I'd be playing the part of Caliban. I didn't have a lot of lines, she said, but I was very important to the play. It was my island before Prospero and Miranda got there. My mother, a witch, had left it to me before she died. My mother had also locked up a fairy named Ariel in a tree. When Prospero came to the island, he set Ariel free. From then on Ariel worked his magic for him. Callahan would be playing Prospero, and Sallie herself was Ariel. It was Ariel who had caused the storm that wrecked the ship, but Sallie stopped reading before I found out why.

Callahan still hadn't come back. "Why don't you go check on him?" Sallie said. "He's probably telling lies or pretending to be somebody he's not."

I slid the silver bowl under the bed, patted Mac one last time, and ran all the way down the stairs to the bar on the first floor. It was too dark to see in right away, so I stood in the cold for a minute and listened to the sound of ice in glasses, a man's loud, slow voice, a woman laughing. The jukebox glowed purple in a corner, and the man behind the bar wore a baseball cap with an A on it. Then the tables appeared out of the dark, each one lit by a candle in a red glass. They were mostly empty, but at one sat a man who had passed out. He wasn't Callahan. I could tell by his bald spot and thickly veined hands.

About the time I'd decided to leave, I saw Callahan at a corner booth with a woman. He was smoking a cigarette instead of his cigar. The woman had coal-black hair and long eyelashes. She wore a silver dress with thin straps that shone in the jukebox's light.

When I walked over, he looked up but didn't seem to recognize me. His face seemed fatter, and his eyelids drooped.

"What's the problem?" he asked.

"It's me," I told him.

"I can see that." He put his arm around my neck and got me in a headlock. "This is my boy here, Rhonda. What do you think of him? He's a good one, ain't he?"

"He's adorable," she said.

"Yeah, adorable," he said. "A little bit unusual, but adorable." He loosened his grip and turned me toward him. "Say, how 'bout doing me a little favor?" he said. "That no-'count bartender gave me gin instead of vodka. Go tell him to fix me what I ordered and bring it over here before I shoot him."

He gave me his glass, and I took it to the bar. The man in the baseball cap said, "That your dad?"

"No. Just a friend."

"Well, you better get him out of here before her husband gets back. They ran out of gas about an hour ago and she's been sitting here while he walks across town to the Conoco. He'd had more than his share too."

He poured the liquor over ice, dropped in a slice of lime, and slid the glass across the bar to me. "I'm not kidding," he said. "That couple causes trouble here all the time. I'd hate to have to use this on either him or your friend." He reached under the bar and pulled out a baseball bat. "You get my drift, don't you? I don't even bother to call the police. I just wade in myself and crack skulls." His smile had a single black tooth in it.

Callahan was sitting alone when I got back. "She's something, isn't she?" he said. "Society woman. Comes here 'cause she likes the low life. I guess that means me." When he leaned close to me, he smelled like something dead. "In case anybody asks, I'm Simonetti, okay?"

"The bartender says you ought to leave before her husband gets back."

"He what?" Callahan's eyes screwed up. "Well, you go back and tell him to mind his own damn business. We're just having a drink."

"I know," I said. "But he's got a baseball bat."

"What's that supposed to mean? Did he send you over here to threaten me? What are you doing down here, anyway? Did Sallie send you to keep an eye on me?"

"She's been reading the play to me. It's getting late."

"I can tell time, you know. And don't you ever, ever mention that play to me. Do you understand?" The woman was coming back. She held on to my chair to steady herself, then sat down.

"I'm covered with dots," she said.

I felt a sharp pain in my side. Callahan was pinching me under the table. I couldn't believe how bad it hurt. "Lizard was just leaving, Rhonda," he said. "Wish him a good-night."

"I'll do better than that. C'mere, let me give him a kiss." I fought off Callahan's hand and raced out of the bar, the woman's laugh chasing after me into the lobby.

Taking the stairs as fast as I could, past all the floors, even the one our room was on, I burst through a heavy green door onto the roof. The air was hot, and I could barely hear the sound of traffic. When I saw the roof wouldn't cave in on me, I walked over to the edge, past a water tank on huge rusted legs, a coiled rubber hose, and a wooden drink case with wilted geraniums in it. Below me the streets looked like they were lying under a red haze. But it was only the neon sign of the Redmont, the heat, and the exhaust from cars that moved like tanks through the deserted streets.

Above me the moon was a yellow quarter. Because of the lights I couldn't see any stars. But for a minute I thought I smelled peaches and woodsmoke. I would have given anything to have heard Rain's voice right then. Or to have felt the sunlight on my arms, like I had when we were walking along the stream, following the faraway song of that bird and thinking any minute we might round a curve and come upon the place where the light began.

The door behind me suddenly opened, throwing a long rectangle of light that nearly touched the edge of the roof. I stepped into the shadow of the water tank and watched as a man staggered to the edge, stopped, and weaved, as though dodging real blows. He was talking to himself, but I couldn't make out the words. Then he lit up a cigar, and I knew it was Callahan.

I stepped into the moonlight. He turned but didn't act surprised. "Wha's up?" he said. He lost his balance and almost sat, but managed to pull himself up by holding to one of the water-tower legs.

"You all right?" I asked.

"Who—"

"Callahan?"

"What are you talking about?" he said.

"It's Lizard."

"I know who the hell you are. And I been meaning to talk to you." When he let go of the water-tower leg, he brushed his hand against his pants. "You're not too bright, Lizard. I mean you are bright, but you're gullible."

"What's that mean?" I said.

"Gullible," he said. The word was like something thick he had to get out of his mouth. He walked toward me, stuffing his hands in his pockets as if to look more natural. But I knew he was dead drunk. "You're a good boy," he said, "but listen to me. That woman what's-his-name was talking about."

"Rhonda?" I said, thinking about what the bartender had told me.

"No, no. The guy at the school. Tinker."

"You mean Miss Cooley," I said.

"That's the one. She's your mother." He smiled a one-sided smile. "See, that wasn't hard. You probably knew anyway."

A car honked. The hot wind shifted. I saw now that the city was a furnace.

"One more thing, and I'll shut up."

I had almost made it to the green door when Callahan whirled me around. His mouth had white flecks of spit in the corners. "Your father's not dead."

"Leave me alone," I said as I pushed him. He fell against the legs of the water tank and slowly slid until he was sitting on the roof.

"He's alive," Callahan said.

10

I WAS OUT of the room with the silver bowl before
Sallie or Callahan woke up the next morning. My plan
was simple. I'd go to the museum and see if the director
would buy the bowl. If he didn't, he could at least tell me
how much it was worth. Then I'd sell it, even if I had to
let it go cheap, and send what I could to Rain's aunt in
Detroit, keeping just enough to buy a bus ticket back to
Louisiana and some cash for food and emergencies. I
didn't care what happened about the play. I'd learned
now that Callahan was a liar and a drunk. The quicker I
could get away from him, the better off I'd be.

The yellow-skinned clerk was asleep at his desk, a bus
driver's cap tilted low over his eyes. When I passed the
bar, all the chairs were on the tables. The bartender was
mopping the floors. I headed straight for the telephone
booth on the corner. In the yellow pages I found out that
the Birmingham Museum of Art was on Eighth Avenue
between Twentieth and Twenty-first streets. The street

sign outside the Redmont said Fifth Avenue North and Twenty-first. It wasn't far, just depended on which direction was which. I walked to the next street sign and discovered I was going south, so I turned around and headed the other way. After a little while I came to the museum, a square marble building trimmed in green.

It hadn't opened yet, so I sat on the steps, putting the bowl, which was wrapped in a paper sack, under my legs. The museum stood across the street from a park. I watched people move through the shadows beneath the trees. Some ran in tight shorts and sweatbands. Others were dressed in suits. I saw a boy about my age being pushed in a wheelchair by a woman with blue hair. He waved at me, his mouth drawing down on one side, and I waved back. We were brothers, all right. Just like me and Mike. If I'd been there when Mike got drowned, maybe I could have saved him. Or maybe we could have gone down together and never come back. I hear it doesn't hurt to die by drowning, just a minute when you're surprised, suck in water, and fall asleep. There wasn't anything to look forward to anyway. Miss Cooley hadn't wanted me. I'd made people unhappy from the start. A bad sign, always underfoot. At the school I was just another boy who beat off too much. And Rain would have forgotten me by now. If she did go away with her aunt, I'd never see her again, and if she stayed in the pump house, the preacher might turn her against me or have me put in jail for stealing the silver bowl. Sallie was the only person I could trust, but she had her own family back in Arkansas, and she was probably planning on having kids with Callahan someday.

I didn't see the old man until he had already climbed the stairs and sat down beside me. His nose was hooked

and his white eyebrows were shaped like wings. "Waiting
for someone?" he asked.

"No."

His eyebrows lifted like they were about to take off.
"Lost?"

"I'm just waiting for the museum to open."

"Oh, that makes sense. It's almost time." He stood up
and took out a key chain.

"Do you work here?" I asked.

"I don't know how much work I do, but I'm down here
a lot." His voice was so faint, I could barely hear him. It
sounded like it hurt him to talk. I watched him fit the key
to the lock and swing the huge glass door inward. The air
inside was cool and still, and when the old man let the
door close behind us, there were no longer any sounds.
He flicked the light switches along the wall. The hall,
which led to a stairwell, lit up, and along either side I
could see the other halls leading away from us, and
through doorways without doors, I could see other
rooms and other halls.

"We're early yet," he said. "Officially, the place
doesn't open till ten, but I like to see the paintings first
thing in the morning, when they're fresh and rested from
the night before. Is this your first visit?"

"Yeah. I'm from Louisiana," I said. "I'm an actor."

His eyebrows lifted again. "Really?"

"That's right." I hoped he'd stop right there.

"My wife was an actress," he said as we turned down a
side hall. I had to listen hard to understand. His voice
had a gentle rasp to it, like the sound a cricket makes.
"She was enormously gifted. It was her particular
beauty." The hall's waxed floors looked like they'd never
been walked on before. The gleaming ashcans along the

wall were filled with clean white sand, and above a narrow strip of woodwork hung picture after picture: flowers, faces, villages, and farms, and some frames with
nothing but colors inside.

He stopped at one room and said, "I think you'll like
this painting."

I knew which one he meant the minute I stepped inside. The entire wall was one big picture of a valley and
mountains and sky, with a shaft of sunlight cutting
through some clouds and falling on a twisted tree sticking out of a creek bank.

"What do you think?" he asked.

"It's great."

He nodded. "The museum is lucky to have it. Someone ran across it in the attic of the downtown library. I
don't think they knew they had it. Can you imagine mis-
placing something like this?"

"What's it a picture of?" I asked.

"Yosemite National Park in California. A painter
named Bierstadt set up his easel by this stream."

"It's something," I said.

"Yes. The trees and boulders, that great expanse of sky
that allows objects to dwindle in significance as they re-
cede in the distance." He had to stop there. All the
talking was wearing him out. But still he had to continue,
as though talking were as valuable as food or sleep. "But
the scene itself," he said so softly, I had to get closer to
hear, "is full of inconsequentials." His face twisted, as
though the word were hard for him to say. "The moun-
tain there, those distant peaks." He dismissed them with
a wave of his hand. "Sure, the valley's impressive, and so
are those delicately drawn poplars and the series of wa-
terfalls that are just trickles now because of the summer

heat. But those things are there right now, and any minute you could get on a plane to California and take a
photo with a Brownie camera and record them yourself.
The reason for the huge and detailed work, these boulders lurching at such crazy angles, the clouds transpar-
ent as curtains in a breeze, is to place a backdrop, a grand
and impressive one to be sure, but still only a backdrop
of mountains and valley and sky for the simple truth of
the entire piece—the way the sunlight falls upon that
single stunted tree." This time when he stopped, I knew
he wouldn't say anything else about the painting. And he
looked like he wasn't really satisfied with what he had just
said. But when I stood back and looked at it good, I
thought I saw what he meant. That painter must have
been crazy to work so hard trying to get that one thing
right.

As if he'd been reading my mind, he said, "It may seem
like a bizarre passion, but that's the effect beauty has on
some men."

He motioned me to sit with him on a padded bench in
front of the picture. "Let me tell you something," he
said, leaning forward, his hands between his knees.
"When World War Two was coming to an end, I crossed
into Germany with the Third Army to rescue whatever
paintings or other pieces of art I could from the churches
and museums along the way."

"Are you the museum director?" I asked.

"Why, yes," he said, as though he'd just remembered
it. "I'm Robert Howell. What's your name?"

"Lizard Sims."

"Good to meet you, Lizard." His eyebrows lifted.
"What was I saying, anyway?"

"The war."

"Yes, the war," he said. "When the war was coming to an end, I had been sent to rescue these pieces of art. I'll never forget the light in those German cities after the armies surrendered. There was a suspension of dust from the ruins, as though from the passage of a great beast. It was a somber twilight in history, I thought to myself. And some of the things I saw—the horribly injured survivors, the bombed-out homes and factories, the swollen corpses in the streets—these things were mirrored in the shredded canvases and blasted statuary. I was terrified by what we had done to ourselves." He looked darkly at the floor, trying to catch his breath. "But there were some paintings still intact, pieces I'd seen before in books and never truly admired, that took on a life quite different now. It was as though they had been meant all along to be viewed in this particular gray light, having survived to remind us of what we had come so close to destroying forever." He looked right at me with his clear blue eyes.

"One day," he continued, "I was searching a burgher's home near Würzburg. There was hardly a wall standing. Yard after yard of exquisite tapestry had been ripped apart and used to wrap the bodies of the dead. But in a music room on a sheltered side away from the force of the Allied bombardment, I discovered a rare and wonderful thing—an unsigned painting by a Master, perhaps Vermeer, of a woman servant in fresh linen, standing before a window, braiding her daughter's hair. I can't explain how the image moved me, except to say I knew with absolute certainty that there was life on the other side of this one. So I gave up my disillusionment with the world and its wars, and with my own life, which had turned into a bitter stalemate by then. And I simply started over with that in mind." He paused. "Am I keeping you from the rest of the museum?"

"The what?" I said. I was still trying to imagine the picture he'd been talking about.

"The museum."

"There's something I want to show you first. It's a silver bowl that belongs to a friend of mine."

"Let's see it," he said. "But I don't remember you bringing anything in."

Then it hit me that I must have left the silver bowl on the steps. "I'll be right back." But when I swung the huge museum door open and looked out into the heat and the noise, I discovered that the silver bowl had disappeared.

11

REHEARSALS started the next day. I tried to put the silver bowl out of my mind. Somebody had stolen it, maybe the boy in the wheelchair, but there was nothing I could do about that. Nothing ever worked out the way it was planned. What I had to concentrate on now was getting paid for being in the play, which opened in three weeks. Then I could take off on my own and get back to Rain.

Sallie and I had a routine that Callahan was in and out of when he pleased. Since the night on the roof I didn't have much to say to him anyway. I was asleep before he came in at night and gone before he woke up the next morning. The room always smelled like bourbon and cigars. At night Sallie read to me and explained what my lines meant in plain English. Then she helped me memorize them. In the morning we rode the bus to the theater so we could get there early and work more on my lines. I never did understand what the individual words meant.

Sallie had given me the gist of it, and that's what I thought about as I learned the words.

I was Caliban. I lived alone on the island my mother had given me until this magician Prospero and his daughter Miranda washed up on the beach one day. They taught me how to read. In return I showed them where to find fresh water and all the good things on the island to eat. I fell in love with Miranda, and when I tried to get her to sleep with me, Prospero set loose a fairy named Ariel on me and turned me into his slave. That was the situation at the beginning of the play. I was supposed to be mad at Prospero, mad enough to kill him. The words came out the way they were in the script because I memorized them exactly that way, but the meaning was something else, something in my head.

Callahan always came to rehearsals late. Sometimes we'd already be in the middle of a scene when Waldo would stop us and say, "Damn it, Cal, get out there. If you miss call again, I'll find another Prospero, even if I have to play him myself. My apologies to the rest of you. Let's take it from the top."

Callahan would always be red-faced and too friendly, his breath smelling like Dentyne over bourbon. He didn't seem like he was in any shape to be in a play, but he'd look quick at his script, stuff it into his pants, take a few deep breaths, and become the magician Prospero.

The first rehearsal without books was the worst. That's when everybody had to leave their scripts backstage. If you forgot your lines, Waldo's wife, Maureen, who was sitting in a folding chair just offstage, would read them loud enough for you to pick back up again. It was good to know that Maureen was there to help me out. But that first time without scripts was one of the scariest moments of my life.

I stayed offstage until Prospero said, "Upon thy wicked dam, come forth!"

Then I walked toward him. We traded a few insults. I had to listen real close for cues. Here's one of them: "Thou shalt be pinched as thick as honeycomb, each pinch more stinging than bees that made 'em."

That's when I said the words that were in the script, but this is what I meant: My mother gave me this island. I was king of it then, and I knew every tree and marsh, where to find blackberries in the summer and where to watch out for wild pigs. There was nothing I couldn't do if I'd wanted to, until you came along and ruined it. I thought you were going to be my teacher. You said you'd teach me how to talk, how to count the shells I found on the beach. But you only taught me enough to know that I was nothing but dirt to you. You wanted the island for yourself. You'd been kicked out of your own place, so you came here to steal mine.

"Move toward him!" Waldo shouted, and I stopped talking. Prospero stepped closer. "That's it. We've got to see you taking charge of your space. Caliban's a dirty little runt, right? You can move in on him any time you want. But don't give any ground yet, Caliban. Keep on telling him off and stay put until he says that about you trying to screw his daughter. Where were we?"

And Maureen got us started again with our lines.

I repeated the words that I'd memorized, but this is what I meant: I can't go to the places that I used to love. You won't let me spend the day looking for heron's eggs or listening to the ocean. I have to work for you and sleep on a rock, and every morning you wake me up and tell me to get to work, get to work. But *you* never work. You don't even enjoy the island you stole from me. Nothing makes you happy except beating me and watching me work.

"Thou didst seek to violate the honor of my child," Prospero said.

I wish I *had* got her, I answered. Then the island would have been full of little Calibans.

"That's where you hit him," Waldo shouted. "Didn't you write that down during walk-through? Somebody throw Prospero his script!"

"Can I borrow a pen?" Callahan asked.

Waldo threw a pencil at Callahan. It hit him in the chest and fell to the floor. Callahan bent over to pick it up and said something under his breath. When he straightened back up, he scribbled in his script, tossed it back offstage, and suddenly became Prospero again. Maureen gave him the cue.

Prospero told me he felt sorry for me and that's why he tried to teach me to talk, but that it wasn't any use. I was too stupid and didn't have any manners.

I said: The only good I got out of learning how to talk was that I can swear at you now, you sorry bastard.

Prospero blew up. He told me to get back to work, and if I didn't, he'd do some magic. Give me a backache or make me sick at my stomach.

So I turned and walked off the stage.

"The limp's great!" Waldo shouted. "Keep it!"

In the dressing room Callahan came up behind me. I could see his lips moving in the mirror. "You sounded like you meant all that."

I didn't say anything. Caliban was a deformed slave who hated his master.

"Come on, Lizard. You haven't even said hello to me today. What's the problem?" He took a wig off a foam dummy's head and put it on, primping in front of the mirror. When he saw that I wasn't smiling, he took off the wig and tossed it onto the table in front of me. I looked at it like it was garbage.

"You don't think I should have been with that woman the other night, do you?" He was pulling his Simonetti act, the big-brother routine. "We were just having some drinks. Sallie didn't care."

"I don't either," I said.

"So what is it?" He had his hands in his pockets. His face was a white triangle. There were smudges under his eyes. "You ran out of the bar like we'd said something that made you mad. We were just having fun."

I didn't look at him. There was makeup on the table, a clipping from the paper advertising pork shoulders. "What about the roof? Were you just having fun up there?"

"Now, that's the part I'm not too clear about," he said. "What was I doing on the roof?"

"You liar," I said. "I'm sick of listening to you. I wouldn't stick around here another minute if I didn't need the money." I got up and headed for the black drape that covered the stage door, making Callahan get out of my way.

When the drape closed behind me, I heard Callahan say, "What's with him?"

Sallie's voice answered, "Somebody stole the silver bowl."

"What are you talking about?" he said.

But I was just believing what I wanted to believe. Miss Cooley was not my mother. And my daddy was dead.

* * *

I slept on the floor next to Mac. His breathing was hoarse and wet. The only light was the square of the window, red and smoky like the city. As opening night got closer, I started having trouble sleeping. My lines from the play went around and around in my head. When Callahan would walk past me to the bathroom, I would stiffen, hoping he wouldn't touch me by mistake. He was drunk every night by the time he went to bed. If he saw me awake, he'd try to talk to me, but I knew better than to listen to his crap.

At the center of me there was a hard spot that hadn't been there before. I was proud of it. Sallie couldn't even soften it when she tried. In a way, I'd already left her and Callahan. I had talked Waldo into loaning me some cash so I wouldn't have to ask Callahan for it. I didn't eat at the hotel, but walked alone through the streets of Birmingham to the Krystal, where the hamburgers were only as big as rolls, or to Walgreen's, where I could get lemonade or a ham and Swiss cheese on rye. Everywhere I went, I practiced my lines and kept an eye out for the boy in the wheelchair. I just knew he had stolen the silver bowl.

Then one day I made the mistake of telling Sallie about the night on the roof with Callahan. She blabbed to him about it, and he came at me after rehearsal. He had a half-empty bottle of bourbon in one hand, and a glass with three ice cubes in the other. "I can't help it when I'm like that," he said. "It's a sickness, sort of. I was passed out, standing up. Don't remember a thing." He poured himself a glass. "So forgive me, okay?" He sipped his whiskey and smiled. "You forgive me?"

"What you said. Was it true?" My voice was coming

from the hard part of me now, the center, so that my lips didn't hardly move.

"Yeah. I saw your records." He tossed back his head, and the bourbon was gone just like that. He sat on the edge of the bed in his dirty T-shirt and jeans, his feet bare. "Next to the word *father* were two boxes," he said. "Living and deceased. The box that said living was checked. I saw it. There weren't any names. But that guy Tinker said Miss Cooley was your mother. That's what he told me, anyway. I acted like I couldn't remember the woman's name."

I was hoping Sallie would get back from the Laundromat soon, because I couldn't stand to look at Callahan when he was like that. "Why didn't you tell me right off?" I asked.

"Look, I didn't even know you thought your father was dead until the night we camped at the peach orchard. Don't you remember? I wouldn't have pretended to be Simonetti if I'd known that." He leaned forward, the bottle dangling between his legs. "Then after I found out, I didn't think it was my place to tell you. I mean, there's a reason why you thought your daddy was dead, wasn't there?"

"Miss Cooley told me."

"That's right. And it's up to Miss Cooley to tell you he ain't." He used the bottle as a counterweight to hoist himself up off the bed. He walked to the window, tried to put a foot on the sill, but couldn't, so he just stood there with his weight on one leg.

I stood up too. "I don't believe a single thing you've said to me since we left Louisiana. Maybe your problem is the whiskey, but that doesn't make what you say true."

"You're the one to talk about truth," he said with that

lopsided smile of his. "Telling Sallie that cock-and-bull
story about a black boy who's really an Indian and that
silver bowl that's supposed to belong to him." He took a
swallow and circled me. "You know as well as me that you
stole that bowl from the preacher, probably right out of
his church when I'd sent you to check the rabbit traps.
No wonder you were gone all day!"

"I told Sallie the truth," I said.

"Sure you did. And about your little girlfriend, that
mythical pickaninny who lives by the stream? Grow up,
Lizard. People outside that state school are too smart to
get conned by thirteen-year-olds like you. I thought you
were a decent kid, but I sure had you pegged wrong. I
can't believe Sallie hasn't seen through you yet. Who in
hell would name a nigger kid Rain?"

I lunged for him before he had a chance to get the
bottle between us. He fell back against the wall with a
thud, and the bottle fell to the floor and broke. I had him
by the T-shirt and skin, and I was shouting at him. I can't
even remember what I said. It'd all been building up, all
the nights waking up out of nightmares to find that nothing at all had changed, Mike drowning just because his
shriveled arm couldn't get him back to the pier, and
Simonetti turning out to be a fake, and the preacher
having his way with Rain, and that boy in the wheelchair
stealing the silver bowl. Most of all it was Callahan with
his lies. Why'd he take me out of the state school, anyway? It was just like waking out of one bad dream and
into a worse one.

He was coughing a little and spitting, his hands up in
front of his face, but then he got up enough energy to
shove me away from him so that I tripped on the leg of

the bed and slid on my butt into the wall underneath the window.

"I've had it with you," he said.

Right then we heard a key in the lock. We both looked toward the door. Mac came in wagging his tail, and then Sallie with a cardboard box full of clean clothes.

"I heard you all the way down the hall," she said, putting the box of clothes on the chair. Her hair had fallen into her face. "Callahan, I need to talk to you alone."

"Let him listen to it," he said. "He needs to know."

"That may be, but there are other things we need to talk about too." She looked from me to Callahan. "Maybe you ought to apologize to Lizard."

"Don't give me that," said Callahan, waving her aside. "Just wait till he's in his thirties and has to unload plumbing supplies all day because nobody's willing to pay him for the only thing he knows how to do."

"That's touching," Sallie said, deadpan. "Lizard, take Mac for a walk, okay?"

I got up off the floor and told Mac to come on. He hid under the bed and wouldn't come out.

"Wait a minute," Sallie said. "I forgot. I found this in your jeans before I put them in the wash." She took out a scrap of brown paper from her shirt pocket. "It's that note from Rain you were telling me about. I didn't mean to read it."

"That's okay," I said, and took it from her, but I didn't look once at Callahan. I just left him in that room in the Redmont like I knew I would someday leave him in real life.

*   *   *

I had walked the three blocks before it struck me where I was headed or why. The art museum was lit by flood-lights like a cemetery vault. When I climbed the stairs, I discovered that the huge glass doors were locked. A black man in a gray uniform and green bandana was mopping the floor. I rattled the cold steel handle. The black man turned around, hesitated, then propped his mop against the wall and unlatched the door. It opened with a rubbery swish.

"We're closed," he said. "Hours are from ten to seven." And he started to shut the door.

"Where's the director?" I said. "He told me he works late sometimes."

"Are you kin to him?" the black man asked.

"No. I'm just a friend."

"A friend," the black man said, nodding slow. "Well, Mr. Howell ain't in."

"Do you know where he is?"

"Now, what business could you have with him on a night like this?" The black man put his hand on his hip, and a necklace with a wooden charm fell out of his gray shirt and dangled against his chest.

"I was thinking about buying a piece of sculpture from him," I lied.

"You were?"

"That's right." I looked frantically into the dim lobby. "That one right there." I pointed to a large wooden crescent anchored to a concrete mound. I had seen it the day I talked to Mr. Howell and had even rubbed my hand across it. It was as smooth as a stone from the bottom of a creek.

"I'll be," the black man said, and walked over to it. "This one right here?" He patted it and then leaned into

it, like a hunter posing with a dead bull. "That's a coincidence, because you know who did this piece?"

"I can't recall right off," I said.

"Huh. Well, let me refresh your memory," he said. "It
was William Tyson, American, 1976."

"Oh, yeah."

"Yes, sir, Willie J. Tyson did this piece. And I ought to
know. Because that's me." He tapped his chest and
laughed.

So he'd caught me. "Okay, I was lying," I said. "I
didn't come to buy anything. I just wanted to talk to Mr.
Howell."

The black man stood straight. "Wait a minute. I don't
think you heard me right. This is really my sculpture. I
did this one and two other pieces that Mr. Howell
bought. And he got me this job at night. Man, I'm set
with food and rent and benefits, and I got use of the
museum studio for free."

I didn't know what to say.

"You still don't believe me, do you?" he said. "Come
on, let me show you the one in the courtyard. It's my
most ambitious. The one I despaired over least. I
thought it was good from the moment of conception,
and I never lost that high. You know, that's rare. Usually,
I hate the piece off and on until it's finished, and then I
just give up on the damn thing."

I followed him across the floor, still damp and streaked
with soapsuds, to a sunken place where there was ground
instead of tile and a window in the ceiling above. The
window opened onto the night. "To appreciate it fully
you got to see it during the day. Sunlight on bronze is a
remarkable thing. I get up there myself to polish that

window with ammonia. But here," he said, turning on
four tiny spotlights.

Each spotlight hit a statue of a girl. They looked so
alive, they startled me. Two of them were standing, and
the other two were just now getting to their feet. The last
to stand up looked a little grumpy, like she'd been woken
from a nap. But the already standing girls didn't seem
sleepy at all. They leaned so close together, their lacy
dresses met. The taller one extended her hand as if to
touch something that she couldn't see. The other had
been caught in the act of looking around, so that one of
her pigtails was suspended in midair. As I walked closer
to them, I saw that their faces were perfectly calm but
struck with a sudden delight, like they were listening to
far-off, joyous music.

"They're about your age," the black man said. "They
were killed in the bombing of a church here in Birmingham in 1963. You remember that?"

"No. That was the year I was born. The year my daddy
died too."

He nodded. "That's the kind of year it was, all right."

"Are they on their way to school?" I asked.

"Oh, no. They were in the church at the time, in Sunday School. This is right after the bomb went off. I call it
'Waking on the Other Side.' "

"Can I touch them?" I asked.

"If you do it with respect," he said.

I hesitated but then couldn't keep away any longer. I
wanted to know what bronze felt like, so I put my fingers
to the inside arm of one of the standing girls, the one
who was feeling the air. It surprised me that something
that looked so warm and alive could be so cool and hard.
I touched a finger to the girl's lips. She took a breath.

The black man laughed when I jumped back. "It's just me. Here I told you to be respectful, and I'm the one playing jokes. Well, I reckon that's poetic license, ain't it?"

I looked from his face to those of the girls. "Did you know them?" I asked.

He shook his head. "I wasn't in Birmingham then. But I tacked their pictures from the newspapers on my bulletin board. Every morning I looked into their faces. The sculpture began to take shape. At the unveiling I met their families. It made me nervous. I didn't know myself whether I hadn't used these girls for my own ends, to further my career, to make a statement at their expense. I was sick all morning, but like with most things, there wasn't any reason to be upset. After the ceremony the families started singing 'Beulah Land.' Everybody wanted to shake my hand. And when the families had left, and this museum had returned to its old cheerless self, I did something uncharacteristic for me, because I had never been a religious man. I offered up a prayer." Then he reached behind his head to tighten his bandana.

"I don't have a family," I said.

"No lie?" He put his hands on my shoulders. "I hope you don't mind me saying this, but you got a very unusual face. What about sitting for me sometime?"

"Sitting?"

"Being a model for me. I'd like to do your head."

"If I'm here that long," I said.

"Well, if you're not, take this anyway." He removed the necklace with the wooden charm and put it around my neck. "You'll find Mr. Howell at the Krystal on Sixth and Twentieth. He always goes there straight from here for pie and coffee and to read the newspaper. If you hurry, you can catch him."

"Thanks," I said. The wooden charm was a miniature crescent just like the sculpture inside the door of the museum.

"You still don't believe I'm a sculptor, do you?" the black man said.

"No," I said, "but I'll try."

He threw back his head. "You'll try. That's great. We'll make a deal. I'll try to be a sculptor, and you try to believe that I am one, okay?"

Mr. Howell was sitting by himself at the counter of the Krystal, his white shirt almost blue in the flat fluorescent light. I eased onto the stool next to him and ordered a glass of orange juice before he turned and saw me.

"What a coincidence," he said. "I've been wondering how to get in touch with you." He folded his paper and laid it beside the half-eaten piece of lemon icebox pie. "You ran out of the museum like it had caught fire."

"I never found the bowl I wanted to show you." The waitress slid the orange juice to me and gave me the once-over with her eyes, which were off center, but not as bad as mine.

"There's a simple reason why you couldn't find your bowl," Mr. Howell said. "It was under the bench by the Bierstadt painting." His smile broadened, and his eyebrows lifted like upside-down V's.

"You found it?" I said.

"You must have slid it under the bench before you sat down."

"I can't believe it," I said, and downed my glass of orange juice. "You see, it's not mine. It belongs to some

friends, and they wanted me to sell it for them, and I
thought somebody had stolen it. Another orange juice!"
I yelled to the woman with off-center eyes.

"Fact is, I've got it in the car," Mr. Howell said.

"How much do you think it's worth?"

"Worth?"

"Worth, worth," I said, so happy my head ached like it
does when I eat something cold.

"It's a beautiful bowl," Mr. Howell said. "I wouldn't
be surprised if you could get at least fifty dollars for it."

"What?" My voice sounded small and hollow to me,
and the blood must have run from my face, because Mr.
Howell looked alarmed.

"Were you expecting more?" he asked.

"But it's silver," I said.

Mr. Howell turned to cough into his hand. When he
looked back at me, his face was soft under the flat blue
light. "No, Lizard, it's not."

I looked at him with first one eye and then the other.
"Sure it is," I said. "What else could it be?"

"I'm sorry," Mr. Howell said. "I assumed you knew it
wasn't silver." He waited until he saw I meant business.
The hard part of me wanted some answers now. "It
seems to be leaded glass with a hard lacquer finish. They
give these bowls away at carnivals and county fairs. For
what it is, it's valuable. There are people who collect
nothing else. But that doesn't help you, does it?"

"Well, I want to see it. Right now. You said it was in
your car, so let's see it." I was off the stool, tugging at his
shirt.

"But I haven't paid," he said.

"I don't care. Come on, let's see the bowl. You said
you had it, right?"

He gave in and motioned to the waitress, who was watching like a frightened hen from the corner between the grill and refrigerator.

Mr. Howell's car was old and silver, with a dent the size of a softball in the left rear fender. I couldn't see what it was he had taken out of the sack until he held it up to the streetlight, and then there wasn't any doubt. As sure as I remembered Rain's face, I knew the bowl. And I knew in the same instant that Mr. Howell was right.

"This must have been important to you," he said. "Is there any way that I can help?"

I had my hands in my pockets as I leaned against the fender. I was watching the shadows on the sidewalk of moths whirling around the streetlight.

"Let's go back inside," Mr. Howell said. "I'll give you a ride back to wherever you live." He put his thin arm around me, and I didn't shrug it off. "It's not the end of anything."

12

"WHERE'S Prospero, damn it?" Waldo said. "He hasn't made a call on time yet."

Callahan smiled his crooked half-smile and raised his hand. He was the only one standing up. The rest of us—me and Sallie and Miranda and Ferdinand, the sailors and dukes and advisers and nymphs—were sitting on the risers or stretching out onstage in our street clothes or costumes. It was seven o'clock on opening night. The curtain went up at eight.

"Listen, all of you," Waldo said. "The play is at a very delicate stage. It could be half decent, or it could embarrass us for the rest of our lives. But it's going on no matter what, so let's remember a few things. Stephano and Trinculo, you're overplaying it in the monster scene with Caliban. Bear in mind who you're working with. Play beneath the kid, not on top of him. And, Prospero, I'm gonna kill you if you blow that last speech again. You've done this role before, so you shouldn't be having these problems this late in the game." Waldo straightened his tie. "All you sailors at the first, remember, you think you're about to die, so act scared! This is a hurricane, you know." He stood up, sweeping his arms in a wide circle and howling like a wild man. "That's me on the tape, by the way. And if I go to that much trouble to scare you, I want you to be scared, understand? Ronnie!" He whirled, like he'd just remembered. "Where was the follow spot in Ariel's big scene?"

"I'm saving it," yelled a voice from the booth in back. "The gels have been melting, and this one's got to last."

"Yeah, well, we haven't had a complete tech yet. The set isn't even finished." He dismissed the entire mess with a wave of his hand.

"What do you want me to do about it?" Ronnie asked.

"All I got to say is that if that follow spot don't follow tonight, your check is going to bounce all over this state." Waldo turned back to us like a dog looking for somebody to bite. "Miranda, I'm telling you one more time. You're not doing a sorority skit. And I noticed a very suspicious glint under the lights today."

Miranda took a silver wire out of her mouth. "Daddy said I'd have to keep it in."

"Those braces have got to go," Waldo said evenly. "I told that to your daddy last night, and I told it to your orthodontist this morning and if it's not out tonight, you won't need it anyway, 'cause you won't have a tooth left to retain. How many times do I have to tell you, there weren't any orthodontists on this island. That's why it was paradise!"

"Waldo?" It was Callahan behind Prospero's gray beard and false nose. "When do we get paid?"

"I thought you were doing this for art," Waldo said.

"But you're right, your performance doesn't come close. The checks, all of them, can be picked up tomorrow at the office. After tonight we split the house, assuming we get a decent review and have a house, which is a way of saying don't count on another dime."

Everybody groaned and started to get up. "Hold it," Waldo said. "A final word. You, too, Prospero. Look, sometimes it's hard for me to say things like this, but I'm proud of all of you for the work you've done. Now just give it plenty of energy. Let it flow. I'll see you tonight at our place after the show."

The dressing room was like recess at the state school. The nymphs were fighting over dresses. The sailors were practicing their lines out loud. Sallie did my makeup in a hurry: some pancake, eyeliner, and a little moist rouge. "Squint," she said, drawing in crow's feet. "Are you and Callahan speaking to each other yet?"

I didn't answer her, because I was Caliban now, the deformed slave.

"I'm worried about him," she said.

I pulled on my burlap shirt and frowned into the mirror. "Do you want to go over lines?" she asked. Her hair was pinned up under a short, peaked cap. Other than that, all she wore was tights and strips of shiny cloth attached to her arms, so that when she whirled and danced, they streamed out behind her. We started with the scene where I come in dragging wood, but before we had gotten far, the music started up in the house, and a voice came through the pipe that connected us to the lobby: "Five minutes."

"We didn't even get a chance to do warm-ups," Sallie

said. "But look at you. I can't believe how calm you are before your first play."

I wasn't calm. I was scared out of my mind.

Maureen breezed through with her clipboard, a cigarette stuck to her upper lip. She made sure that everybody in the first scene, the storm, was lined up at the stage door. Some of them did knee bends or toe touches. One of the sailors, a red-haired boy with big lips, looked like he was praying.

"How's the house?" Callahan asked.

Maureen shrugged. "Maybe there'll be some late shows. We're holding a minute while they rewire the light board. They're soldering and everything. The whole place stinks." She dragged on her cigarette and scribbled furiously on her clipboard.

"Do I have time to look out there?" I asked.

"Do whatever you like. Just don't let the audience see you."

I tiptoed down the hall separating the dressing room from the stage. The drapes there were pinned with safety pins, and I undid one and peeked out. When I saw the faces, I felt like I might get sick. I could count the teeth of the man in the front row. He had sweat beneath his nose, and the woman next to him wore a man's sport coat with a missing button on the sleeve nearest me.

"Lizard! We're ready," someone whispered, and I made my way back past the sailors and lords and dukes.

"Are you okay?" Sallie asked me.

"I'm going to throw up."

She led me to the bathroom. It was tilted at a crazy angle, so I had to get on my knees.

"I'll get a wet towel," she said.

I put my cheek on the cold toilet seat while the music for the play wound around in my head. There were flutes and another instrument that sounded like a duck. It sounded like the duck was chasing the flutes and the flutes were crying for help. All I could think was that if the music didn't stop, I'd throw up. When I started to spit in the water at the bottom of the toilet, I saw part of my reflection. I looked at myself with first one eye and then the other and wondered how I'd gotten into the mess I was in.

Sallie wrapped the wet towel around my head. "Are you going to make it?" she said.

I wasn't sure, but I nodded anyway. Then the music stopped. I heard the familiar roaring of the storm, and the first words of the sailors, which I had heard so often in rehearsals, I knew by heart. My head began to clear. It's just like a rehearsal, I thought, and that seemed to help.

Slowly I stood up. Maureen came rushing into the bathroom. "Ariel, what are you doing in here? You're on!"

Before she left, Sallie adjusted her cap, squeezed my hand, and said, "Break a leg."

"You too," I said, and I could hear Miranda's voice from the stage: "If by your art, my dearest father, you have put the wild waters in this road, allay them. . . ." I wondered if her braces were out. And then I heard Callahan, playing Prospero, his voice now old and deep. "Be collected. No more amazement," he said. I didn't know what my first line was going to be, but I didn't care. It was too late. I felt like I was asleep and dreaming about a play. The lines were going faster than they ever had in rehearsal. Already Sallie, as Ariel, had leapt upon the stage, and Maureen was urging me down the hallway.

I tried to remember what Waldo had been telling us, about getting into character, getting into character. I am Caliban, I thought as I waited in the hall, and I practiced cocking my head the way Caliban did his, and I smiled a Caliban smile.

"What ho! Slave! Caliban! Thou earth, thou! Speak!"

Now I knew there was no way out. So I yelled, too fast and too loud, from offstage: "There's wood enough within."

Prospero laughed a cold laugh. "Thou poisonous slave, got by the devil himself upon thy wicked dam, come forth!"

And before the words were said, I was through the drapes that Maureen held back for me, into the lights, and face-to-face with Prospero for the first time.

My lines came to me as though there was a voice deep in the back of my head. I didn't think about the audience or the lights. The set was gleaming with fresh paint—the cave, the fire, and the beach—but I didn't really see all those things. I didn't even think about what was supposed to happen next. I just listened to what Prospero was saying and concentrated on his face. His eyebrows were arched and his lip curled like the sight of me made him sick.

". . . thou shalt be pinched as thick as honeycomb," he said, "each pinch more stinging than bees that made 'em."

And I picked up my cue without knowing I had done it. The words just poured out of my mouth. But the meaning was something else, something deep inside my head.

Then it happened.

"Thou most lying slave . . ." Prospero interrupted. I hadn't said his cue. He had come in too soon, and something behind his eyes changed. "Thou most lying slave . . ." he said again. He gestured with his hand in a way he never had in rehearsals. Something was wrong. I felt a rush of panic. Prospero had forgotten what came next!

"Abhorred slave," Miranda suddenly blurted out, and I knew she'd skipped ahead. It was a long speech, and I fought to get back into character, so I'd be ready to jump on the cue she gave me at the end: "Therefore wast thou deservedly confined into this rock, who hadst deserved more than a prison."

And I did. I jumped on my cue. But Prospero just looked at me funny like I hadn't said the right thing. "Thou most lying slave . . ." he said again.

We circled each other while Miranda watched with a look of horror and alarm. I broke out in a sweat. It was like we were on a sinking ship. Where was Maureen? I thought. In rehearsals, when something like this had happened, she'd calmly said a line from offstage and gotten us back on the right track. But I knew she wasn't back there now. I could see her clearly in my mind's eye, sitting on the steps outside the dressing room fire exit, smoking a cigarette. And I could tell that the audience knew now just how wrong things had gone. There was a restlessness in the back rows. A woman in the front coughed, and someone else stifled a laugh.

I tried not to look into Prospero's eyes, afraid what I would see in them, but I couldn't avoid them altogether. "Thou most lying slave . . ." he said for the fourth time, and then I saw them. They were Callahan's eyes, defenseless and terrified. They were the eyes of a man who suspects he's just been set on fire.

What happened next I can't explain. I tried to start my lines over again from my entrance, but I didn't get very far before the words that came out were not the lines I'd memorized. They were what the lines meant deep in the back of my head, and they tumbled out the way I thought Caliban would have said them.

"So that's how my lessons began," I said. "In payment I took you all over the island. I showed you where the herons nested, where the deer drank at the stream. And everywhere we went, you named things for me. Sometimes you or Miranda sang. And soon I even knew words for things I'd never seen. Like love."

Callahan's eyes latched on to mine. "Poisonous wretch," he said, struggling to become Prospero again.

"At night I tried to sleep," I continued. "But the words tumbled around in my head." I paused. "I could think, but I didn't know whether thinking was a gift or a curse. For all I could think about was love."

Callahan sputtered something and shook his head. His sweat flew in beads under the lights.

"I'd lost my kingdom for love," I said, stepping toward him across the sand. "And what good was the knowledge you'd given in return? What good was knowing the word for love without knowing the thing?"

Callahan turned away. He took a shuddering breath, and when he turned back around, his eyes had become Prospero's again.

"Get to work before I tell Ariel to pinch you to death," he said.

"But what about my lessons?" I asked.

"You know too much for your own good already," he said.

"But the names of the seasons. You haven't told me yet."

"What for? It's wasted on you. You're as . . . you're as dense as a swamp."

"And the stars," I said. "You were going to tell me about the stars."

There was a silence. If it had been planned, Waldo would have called it a beat. During it a voice from off-stage whispered: "Hagseed, hence."

Prospero tilted his head.

"Hagseed, hence," the voice whispered again. It sounded like Maureen.

Prospero suddenly unfurled his cape and in a booming voice said, "Hagseed, hence! Fetch us in fuel. And be quick, thou'rt best . . ." And like a record player that had been turned from long playing to 45, the play was up to speed again.

"What happened out there?" Sallie asked in the dressing room. She was reapplying dry powder to her cheeks.

"Callahan forgot his lines," I said. The rest of the chairs were taken up by frantic nymphs.

Maureen brushed by at just that moment. "Good work," she said, and patted me on the shoulder. "We don't use prompters during performances, so it took me a while to find the place."

The other actors were gathering around. "You mean he just blanked out?" one of them said.

"God, I'd just die if that happened to me," someone else said.

"It was *terrible,*" Miranda began, "like these dreams you have about walking into a party naked."

"That doesn't sound so bad to me," said one of the sailors.

"Pipe down!" Maureen snapped. "They can hear us back here. Intermission's almost over. Five minutes. Places for Act Two."

"Are you going to be all right?" Sallie asked me.

"Sure."

Callahan entered from the wardrobe closet. He had changed into another tunic, and he was toweling the sweat off his face. When he saw me, he stopped long enough to mouth the word *thanks* over the heads of the sailors and nymphs.

And the rest of the play went all right, I guess, except for the electrical cable that started smoldering during my scene with Trinculo and Stephano. I don't think the audience noticed. They probably thought it was special effects. I never did get my concentration back all the way, but I didn't blow any lines, and I felt this odd, what Waldo would call "chemistry" between Prospero and me, so that by the time he reached his final speech it was almost like he was addressing it to Caliban more than anybody else.

After the blackout the stage lights came on. We took our bows exactly like Waldo had told us, in pairs. Ariel and I came right before the lovers and Prospero. At the end we all joined hands. The seats in the theater were half empty, but the audience applauded a pretty good while, long enough for us to take two curtain calls. And then the houselights came up and Sallie was hugging me and telling me what a great job I'd done, and I caught a glimpse of Callahan out of the corner of my eye. He was peeling off his fake eyebrows and placing them ever so carefully in his makeup kit, as though he was turning something over in his mind, something that would take more courage than he thought he had.

13

ON THE WAY to the cast party at Waldo and Maureen's, Callahan didn't say a thing. But Sallie couldn't contain herself. She thought we'd done a great job, given the short rehearsal time and the shape the theater was in and the age of some of the actors and actresses. "Not you, Lizard," she added immediately. "You were just like a veteran out there."

But she knew that the Birmingham reviewers wouldn't like the play. "Shakespeare invites a kind of snobbishness, even in places where there's nothing to be snobbish about. Who cares what they say, though? It's a super show, don't you think, Cal?"

He nodded.

"A very fine show," she added, a bit wistfully.

Cars lined the street for two blocks in front of Waldo and Maureen's house. It was one of those big Southside houses that we'd seen our first day in Birmingham. It had high ceilings and a curving staircase and a wraparound porch, but it seemed a little run down. The wallpaper had come loose in the living room, there were stains on the ceiling from a leak in the bathtub upstairs, and a broken window in the kitchen had been replaced with the end panel from a cardboard box. All in all I felt right at home.

The rest of the cast was in a great mood. Miranda and Ferdinand were trying to jitterbug next to a portable stereo blaring "Born to Be Wild." One of the nymphs was bent back almost double while she danced under a broom. But nobody was talking much about the play. It was more like a going-away party than an opening of something. I think we all knew there wouldn't be another performance. Waldo had already said almost as much. But nobody wanted to admit it just yet. It would spoil everybody's fun.

When Sallie got me alone in the kitchen and told me she wouldn't be going back to Louisiana with us, she made it sound like Callahan and me would have fun. Her eyes were bright. "Callahan needs you," she told me. "And I guess right now you need him."

"I thought you wanted to meet Rain," I said.

"I do, but I can't be two places at the same time. I need to spend some time with my family in Arkansas. You understand."

Callahan came into the kitchen just then. His skin was gray and bloodless, and his hair stuck out to the side. He poured another glass of ice water—I don't think he'd touched a real drink all night—and leaned into the wall by the refrigerator, like he was shy and had forgotten how to have a good time.

"I didn't know the party was back here." Miranda giggled from the doorway. Her upper lip was purple with wine, and her braces were back in.

"It's not," Callahan said. Miranda stood for a minute longer anyway, and then disappeared into the dining room, where Waldo and Maureen were singing a duet.

"So what's the verdict?" Callahan asked.

"He's going with you," Sallie said.

"Good." Callahan ducked his eyes. "I'm sorry about the way I've been. About the bowl and the girl and all. What's her name?"

"Rain," I said.

"Rain," he repeated, and seemed to stare at a spot on the kitchen tile. "I just hope we can find the orchard."

"It's twelve miles east of Newllano," I said. "Don't you remember clocking it?"

Callahan looked up. His eyes were red-rimmed. He must have been thinking something else. When he tried to take another drink of water, the glass shook. "What time is it?" he said.

Later he went to sleep on the porch swing without even taking off his shoes. I didn't know what to make of him. Callahan had caused a part of me to harden inside. I had needed it as a defense against him and his lies. But asleep on the porch swing, grimacing like he was in the middle of a bad dream, he didn't seem capable of arousing anybody's defenses. In ways, he must have always been worse off than me.

"Evening, Lizard," a voice said.

I turned to see Mr. Howell sitting in a wheelchair pushed by Willie Tyson, the black man who had been mopping the floors at the museum. Behind them the party was still in full swing.

"What are you doing here?" I asked.

"I always come to opening nights," Mr. Howell said in his soft, rasping voice.

"I designed the set," Willie Tyson added.

"You did?"

"Will you please tell this boy that I am really an artist?" he said to Mr. Howell, who merely smiled and said, "The best."

"I believe you," I said.

"He saw me cleaning up and assumed that I was the museum's hired help."

"Aren't we all?" Mr. Howell said.

"You do whatever it takes to buy time for your real work," Tyson said. "You understand?"

"Sure," I said, and I glanced at the footrests of the wheelchair.

"Don't let this worry you, Lizard," Mr. Howell said. "Sometimes I'm weak after my chemotherapy. I've got a touch of throat cancer, you know. It's more a bother than anything else."

"A real nuisance," Willie said. I stood aside while he maneuvered the chair through the doorway and onto the porch.

"By the way, I thought your Caliban was wonderful," Mr. Howell said. It was then I noticed a pair of binoculars in his lap. "You told me you were an actor, but I didn't place you with Waldo's group. The program confused me. Is Jerry Koswinski your stage name?"

"He's the guy I replaced. I'm not really an actor," I said. "This is the first play I've ever been in."

"Well, you're off to a good start."

"You just about cracked me up in that first scene," Willie Tyson added.

"It wasn't meant to be funny," I said.

"So?" he said. "You take what you can get."

Mr. Howell lifted the binoculars from his lap. A sliver of new moon had risen above the housetops. I figured that was what he had in mind to look at. Next to the moon was a star so bright, it seemed to cast a light over the lawns and clipped hedges. The cicadas were singing like mad. Callahan snored once, and Maureen appeared at the door. "Everything all right out here?" she said. "Can I get you boys anything?"

"No, thank you, dear," Mr. Howell said. He was adjusting the eyepieces on his binoculars, his eyebrows knitted. Willie Tyson and I shook our heads, too, and Maureen disappeared again into the din of the party.

"Jupiter is in conjunction with the moon tonight," Mr. Howell said. "I wanted Willie to take a look, to put to rest a metaphysical argument we have been having, but I can't get the blooming thing to focus. See what you can do, Willie." He passed the binoculars on.

"What am I looking for?" Willie said.

"Try focusing on the moon first."

"I got it. Say, that's not bad."

"Is it in focus?" Mr. Howell said.

"For my eyes it is. Wow, you can see the shadows of the lunar mountains."

"Okay, now look to the right, at that bright star."

"Uh-huh."

"That's Jupiter."

"Huh. Looks like just a star to me," Willie said.

"I know, but trust me. It's Jupiter. Now, to the right of Jupiter you should be able to see two faint pinpoints of light." His voice was almost a whisper.

"What say?"

"I say if you look to the right of Jupiter, the northeast

quadrant, you should be able to see two very faint points of light."

We waited while Willie Tyson adjusted the right eye-piece. Behind us the noise of the party had swelled, and above it someone was singing loudly and painfully off key. "Maybe it's my imagination," Willie said, "but I think I see what you're talking about. They're like in a line at about a forty-five-degree angle from the planet?"

"That's them," Mr. Howell said. "Let Lizard have a look."

I didn't know what to do with the binoculars.

"I see your problem there," Willie said.

Mr. Howell turned his head. "What's that?"

"Somebody needs to make binoculars for people with eyes like Lizard's. Maybe some kind of extension with mirrors."

"It's okay," I said. "I can take them one at a time." I tried every combination, but the focus was better with my right eye on the left eyepiece. After staring awhile, though, I told them I couldn't see anything to the right of Jupiter.

"Try looking a little more to the side," Mr. Howell said. "Distant lights are brighter when viewed peripherally."

"What does that mean?" I asked.

"Sometimes things are clearer when you don't look at them head on," he answered.

I did what he suggested, and for an instant I thought I saw what he and Willie were talking about, two dim pinpoints that seemed to disappear when I looked directly at them. "I think I saw them," I said. "Are they stars or planets?"

Mr. Howell settled into the wheelchair. "Those are two of the moons of Jupiter."

"You're kidding," Willie said. "Let me take another look."

I passed him the binoculars. I didn't even know other planets had moons.

"The moons of Jupiter," Willie repeated with a smile. "So they revolve around Jupiter the same way the moon revolves around the earth. This is better than high-school physics."

Callahan, still asleep, flung his arm over his head, causing the swing to shimmy on its chains.

"The observation is an important one," Mr. Howell said, and Willie and I leaned close on either side of him to hear. "Galileo was the first person we know of to see the moons of Jupiter. He took them as proof that Copernicus's theory was right."

"Uh-huh," Willie said. "And what theory was that?"

"That the universe doesn't revolve around us." Mr. Howell's eyebrows lifted like wings.

The party went on long after Willie and Mr. Howell had gone home. The actor who had played the king of Naples suggested a ring dance in the street to celebrate sunrise. But Waldo wanted me to ride with him downtown instead, where we shivered in the dawn waiting for the first morning papers to come off the presses and onto the trucks. Then we had breakfast at the farmers' market —fresh cantaloupe, scrambled eggs with hot sausage, and grits. Waldo folded the paper in front of him so he could read the review while he ate.

"Are you interested in hearing any of this?" he said.

"Sure."

"Okay, but bear in mind two things," Waldo said. "First, the production was beautiful, and I'm not saying that just because I directed. Second, this particular reviewer has personal problems that are not worth going into right now."

"So what does he say?"

"The headline is TEMPEST IN A TEAPOT. Very original, don't you think?"

Then Waldo began to read: " 'The most riveting performance in Southside Repertory Company's production of *The Tempest* was turned in last night by a lighting cable that overheated and threatened to burst into flame midway through the second act. By contrast the play itself was an utter bore, despite the able gymnastics of Sallie Petrie's Ariel and flashes of energy from a youthful supporting cast. . . .' Blah blah. 'The decision by director Waldo Stakes to inaugurate SRC's new space—a former delicatessen kitchen, we are told (and believe)—with Shakespeare remains a mystery. Surely, it will be a financial debacle. How much more practical and aesthetically pleasing it would have been to start with one of those delightful musical revues that have charmed this reviewer for years. . . .' Give me a break," Waldo said.

"What'd he say about Callahan?" I asked.

"Uh, let's see. . . . 'Prospero wore the look of a man trapped by insufferable odors.' He owes Flannery O'Connor for that one," Waldo said.

"That's all?"

"That's it about Prospero. Oh, here's something that might interest you: 'Hats off, though, to the makeup crew for the bang-up job they did on Jerry Koswinski's Caliban. We remember Jerry from last summer's production of *Dark of the Moon,* and we almost didn't recognize him behind his beautifully grotesque mask.' "

"Mask?" I said.

Waldo shrugged and set the paper aside. "Critics. Aren't you glad they're around to mold the public taste?"

"I guess so." I had thought the question was serious.

"Look, Lizard," Waldo said. He had folded his hands on the table. "Maureen and I don't have any kids around the house. You're free to stick around with us if you'd like."

If it hadn't been for Rain, I might have taken him up on that.

14

TWELVE MILES east of Newllano it began to rain. Callahan pulled onto the shoulder of the road. Nothing looked familiar, but we were stopping anyway. He cut the engine, and the windshield wipers died with a screech. "We'll go till we find the stream and follow it," he said, pouring from a thermos of coffee while we waited for the rain to slack up. I was still working on the Coke I'd gotten at the last Texaco. Callahan knew what I wanted to ask him. He'd told me the whole trip not to think that far ahead. "We'll take Rain and Sammy with us," he said when I started to speak. And when I asked about the preacher, he said, "No preacher ever stopped me from doing anything."

His eyes were small and hard as he blew across the cup. He'd been on edge since Alabama, but it was better than when he'd been drunk.

"Did Sallie leave because of me?" I asked.

"Shoot, no. She's visiting her family and taking a rest. She'll probably be in Houston before we are."

"Why'd she take Mac, then?"

"Mac's her dog, Lizard. Don't you understand? Now, give me a break about Sallie." He took a sip.

"It's hot in here," I said.

When Callahan cranked the side window open, I could smell the rain. We'd watched the storm for miles as it spread across the western sky like a slow, dark stain. From Vicksburg on there hadn't been any thunder, just heat lightning tinged with green. I took the last sip of Coke, rolled down the window on my side, and threw the bottle into the weeds.

"Everything's grown up," I said.

Callahan was thinking about something else. "I'd like to see that preacher's face," he said.

"He beats them," I said.

"I know."

"And he has his way with Rain." I watched him take another sip, the steam from the coffee hanging in the air like a veil. "You believe me, don't you?"

Callahan looked at me. "If I didn't believe you, I wouldn't be here." He poured the rest of his coffee out the window. "It's slacking," he said. "Want to try it?"

My hand was on the doorknob, but I wanted to know whether Sallie was really coming back.

"I told you," Callahan said as he screwed the thermos tight.

It was still sprinkling when we got out. "Look familiar?"

I shook my head.

"Me either. But we can't go wrong if we head straight in. Let's keep about a hundred feet apart, and whoever sees the stream first, yell." He walked a ways and then turned around and said, "She'll be okay."

I nodded, but I didn't know whether he meant Sallie or Rain.

I came out of the orchard and into the pine trees just as the rain completely stopped. The air was cooler here, like I'd remembered from before. The sun shone in patches on the wet ground. I followed a path the water had cut down the hill, slipping now and then in the soft red mud. A pair of goldfinches shot in front of me, and a butterfly tried to light on my arm.

"Callahan!" I yelled, for I couldn't hear him now. The only sound was the dripping from the trees.

The path I was following had run into a ditch that was too small to be the stream, but I walked with the current, hoping the ditch might widen and dip beneath the pump house where Rain and Sammy lived. But it petered out in a rutted road that led back up to another orchard. I looked for Callahan between the rows, but I didn't see him and he didn't answer my calls.

Then it happened that I reached a spot that seemed familiar to me. I stopped, like I must have done before, and tried to figure out whether I really remembered the place. Then it hit me that this was where I'd seen the fox in the path and had stopped until it took off like a spark into the trees. I yelled again for Callahan and waited until the silence answered me back. As though following the fox's ghost I slipped into the pines again and made my way downhill until I found what had to be the stream. Every turn seemed familiar, though I tried not to get my hopes up too far. If I'd learned anything since I left the state school, it was that things never work out the way they're planned, and I didn't want to think I was heading for the pump house if this stream, too, was going to dead-end. But I couldn't help feel something rise in me, for the stream looked as though I'd never left. The water level was the same on the stumps. And it seemed those were the same gnats rising from the surface and the same mockingbirds courting in the bushes along the bank. When I came to a place where the stream took a turn, I could tell by the light that a clearing was ahead, and so I wasn't surprised when I rounded that bend and discovered the stretch of weeds where Callahan had set the rabbit traps. Beyond the weeds stood the pump house, with its tin roof reflecting what there was of the sun.

I half expected to hear Sammy's voice behind me, wanting to know what I thought I was doing there, but even at that distance, in the stillness of the clearing, I knew the pump house was empty and had been for a while.

The door flapped open and shut. I looked inside. The stove was gone. So were the chairs and the crowbar I'd thought was a gun and the snakeskins tacked to the wall and the books. The place smelled like a fire had gone out there a long, long time ago.

I stood in the doorway, looking out at the stream and beyond it the pine trees and orchard and sky. "Rain?" I yelled as loud as I could.

"There's nobody here," a voice replied.

I walked to the spot where we had swum naked under the trees, and there sat Callahan with his back to the pump house. He was chewing a long, brittle weed.

"I swear they used to live here," I said.

Callahan sat in silence, staring out across the stream.

"This is where we swam," I went on. "Rain told me

how her mother disappeared in the flood." I looked past Callahan's face to the deeper pine woods beyond. "She took me to the cave, where Sammy was digging out the passageway that had been blocked. And then we drank from the silver bowl and sat on the steps till it got dark." But even as I told him about it, the memory began to fade like a dream. Only the woods were solid and real now. Nothing living moved except a hawk, who glided in circles that stretched farther and farther downstream.

"It's getting late, Lizard," Callahan said. "We'd better go back to the truck."

It was Callahan's idea to go to the courthouse in De Ridder and talk to the deputies who'd stopped us on the road and been with the preacher where we camped. They'd know where to find the preacher, or at least his name, which was more than we knew now. He'd have to tell us about Sammy and Rain. The only problem was that the deputies might still be looking for me.

Luckily, we remembered the costumes and makeup and wigs in the truck. We decided the people most in need of a preacher would be a couple who wanted to get married. So Callahan put on his fake nose and mustache, Mr. Simonetti's glasses, and a blue pinstriped suit. I wore one of Sallie's dresses, a blond wig, and a pair of wrap-around sunglasses we found on the sale rack at Thompson's Seed and Feed. At the last minute we put a bandage over my nose.

Then we walked to the Beauregard Parish courthouse, which was next to the old parish jail. My high-heeled shoes were killing me, but I tried to just think about putting one foot in front of the other. Callahan opened the door and said, "After you, dear." The sheriff's office was to the left down a dim hall that smelled like wet telephone books.

"Hep you?" the woman dispatcher asked, but before Callahan could think what to say, the deputy with cauliflower ears stepped out of an office and threw a sheaf of papers on the dispatcher's desk.

"Hold it a minute, Roger," she said. "You still got to sign this one on top."

"That one there is Homer's," he said. "I didn't have nothing to do with that."

"But Homer's on vacation, and somebody's got to sign it. What do you think the sheriff's gonna say?"

"Come on, Louise, don't make me sign my name to that. I didn't requisition no tear gas grenade launcher. When in hell would we ever use one of them?"

"It's already been ordered."

"That's not my fault. Homer would order a tank if he thought the sheriff wouldn't turn him down."

The dispatcher turned her huge eyes on us, but the deputy had already seen us by now. "What can I do for you folks?" he asked.

"Just some information that would make me the happiest man in the world," Callahan said.

The deputy straightened his tie. "Rest room's down the corridor past the automobile tags."

Callahan laughed and took my hand. "I'm afraid you misunderstand," he said. "This is my fiancée, Miss Sarah Wills. And I'm Rudy Simonella, from Baton Rouge."

The deputy seemed struck by this. "Haven't I met you before?"

Callahan cringed. "Don't believe so."

"Something about a dog?"

"Dog?" Callahan looked quizzically at me. I thought a minute and shook my head.

"My memory's as sharp as a tack," the deputy said. "It'll come to me bye and bye."

"I hope so," Callahan said. "I always enjoy renewing an old acquaintance. But meantimes, Sarah and myself are itching to get married this afternoon if we can find a dear old black preacher who married Sarah's mom and dad."

"What's his name?" the dispatcher asked, turning her large eyes on me. "Maybe I can hep."

"Now that's the very thing. We forgot to ask. And both of Sarah's folks are dead now."

"Poor thing," the dispatcher said.

"Yes, ma'am. But in their fond recollections of the man they mentioned one thing that ought to give him away." Callahan lowered his voice. "He only has one eye."

The deputy dropped his gaze, and the dispatcher returned to her paperwork with a sigh. "You folks don't want *him* to marry you," the deputy said.

"You know him, then?" Callahan even fooled me, he acted so surprised. "Why, that's a lucky coincidence, ain't it, sweetheart?"

I smiled behind my wraparound sunglasses.

"I don't believe you heard me," the deputy continued, picking up his hat from the dispatcher's desk and polishing its vinyl brim with his thumb. "You don't want him marrying you."

"Of course we do," Callahan said. "Is he all booked up?"

"You might say that, mister. He's booked, all right." The deputy put on his hat, adjusting it by looking in the window of the door behind us. "He's cooling his heels in this very jail."

Callahan shook his head sadly. "Sarah's folks admitted that he drank a bit more than he should, but that's all right with us. We're only interested in preserving a family tradition. If we could talk with him, maybe we could schedule the ceremony after he gets out."

The dispatcher stopped her paperwork and stared across the room at a calendar with a duck-hunting scene, although this was summer instead of fall. And the deputy, sensing that he was performing an unpleasant official duty, said, "He can't see no visitors. That's parish policy when there's a capital offense involved."

I felt a quickening in my stomach then, and my arms broke out in goose bumps. Callahan's cold wet hand let go of mine.

"What are you talking about?" he said, but this time in his own voice.

"I wish it weren't nothing but public intoxication," the deputy continued. He hitched his trousers and squared his shoulders. He was all business now. "I'm afraid the Reverend Ephraim Smith is charged with a much more serious crime."

Callahan must have known then what had happened. He motioned me to sit down, but I wouldn't budge. "What's the charge?" he finally asked.

"That he did willfully murder, or cause to be murdered, one black female who lived in an orchard on his property east of Newllano."

15

PEOPLE CAN take almost anything. And though I hadn't reasoned this out at the time, the hard part of me, the part that grew out of my not trusting Callahan—that part lay right under the surface like a rock. I didn't like it, but I knew it would be a useful weapon if I had to keep going through life alone.

Callahan and I didn't talk about such things. We didn't talk that night at all. What I knew was that there were two hundred steps from the courthouse to the truck, which was parked next to Thompson's Seed and Feed. I knew there were seven buttons on the truck radio, a round speedometer that went to one hundred and ten. I knew the fourth traffic light was the last one on Pine, and that the boardinghouse where we stopped had three lighted windows on the second floor, even though it didn't have a name. I only saw the word ROOMS written in green paint on a heavy rusted chair on the front lawn. I didn't know how we got up the stairs to our room, but I did know there were fourteen steps, and the light was on under the door of room number two, and the bathroom in the hall contained a single bulb hung from a metal chain.

I knew there'd come a time when I'd be able to think about the orchard and the girl who lived in the pump house. But that night I only thought that there were two yellow pillows under the sheets, and that Callahan sat at the open window until four, and that I didn't go to sleep until after that. Even then, my sleeping was just one dream after another, each one flat and full of heat. I dreamed I was looking at myself in a mirror, and my reflection turned and walked away from me. I dreamed I was in a funeral home with bodies stretched out under sheets. Some of them were moving, and I was alone. When I woke up, there was a wet, sour spot on my pillow.

The light in the hall was on. I staggered out in my underwear. Voices came from another room, and a moth dove again and again at the light. I listened to the voices but couldn't make out any words. In the bathroom I watched it get light, looking out below on a yard with weeds as high as the first-floor window, and a yellow dog with a mange-eaten tail. He was tied to a mimosa tree, but had wrapped his chain around a concrete birdbath and lay panting in the weeds with his neck crooked because of the tangled chain. The copy of *Sports Afield* beside the toilet was dated April 1974. In the soap dish were two bars of Lifebuoy soap, stacked one on top of the other. The dog started yelping like somebody was slowly breaking his neck. I looked over the sill, and the woman who had given us the key to the room, a white-haired woman with garters that had come loose from her hose, was dragging a washtub across the yard. She carried a long stick in her other hand.

"Ramón!" she yelled. "Ramón, you sit! Sit!" She left the washtub in the weeds and untangled the dog from the birdbath. He slinked behind the mimosa tree and took a leak, looking back at the woman as if she might hit him with her stick. But she was poking it now into a compost heap, her other hand scratching her rear.

When I flushed the toilet, a pool with hair and rust rose out of the drain in the tub, and I watched it gurgle back. I splashed water on my face, looking at myself with first one eye and then the other. When I went back to the room, Callahan was sitting in the chair by the window, just like he'd been all night. Staring at what? I wanted to know, but it wasn't worth my time.

"We got to eat something," he said, like that was the last straw.

We drove to the Texaco by Thompson's Seed and Feed, where there was a counter with three stools and a rack of deviled ham sandwiches. We split one and each had a Coke. The guy behind the counter wore a Texaco cap and overalls. He watched us like a hawk. "Mighty hot," he said.

We finished our sandwich and Cokes. "Take out for a pack of M&M's and keep the rest," Callahan said. He handed the man two ones and a Kennedy half. Then he passed me the M&M's and stood examining the labels on cans of oil. I found an old mileage chart tacked to the wall, the southeast U.S.A., with circles drawn like a target, the bull's-eye at Baton Rouge. With a ballpoint pen somebody had connected three dots—De Ridder, Leesville, and Newllano, La.—and made the line into a stick figure. The M&M's were hard, stale. I tossed them into a barrel filled with oily paper towels and crumpled Lucky Strike packs. I had the feeling that I was nowhere, that time had stopped and the real world melted away. Beneath it there was this gas station, and beyond it the brittle yellow light that covered everything exactly the same. Callahan walked up beside me. He was thumbing through an old Christmas catalog but looking straight ahead. "How you feeling?" he asked. He needed a shave.

"All right," I said. I'd rather have been dead.

"Did you get enough to eat?"

"Yeah."

"It's eight-thirty. We better get over to the courthouse."

The preacher was due to be arraigned at nine. The deputy had told us that much. I didn't want to have to look at him, but I had to give the silver bowl to Sammy, and I figured he'd be there.

Outside the heat settled on us in an instant. There wasn't any wind. Already the asphalt steamed and the sidewalks looked buckled from the heat. The courthouse was next to the old parish jail, which had rows of barred windows and a bell tower. I could see the hands around the bars in the single window beneath the tower, and I wondered if they were his—the man who had murdered Rain.

It was the first time I'd allowed myself to think the thought all the way through, and it left me with nothing else to think. It'd be this same street from now on out. The heat wouldn't ever lift. I didn't worry about what to say to Sammy, because there wasn't anything to say.

We sat on the courthouse steps. A car pulled up—a black Ford Fairlane with an old farmer and his wife. The man wore suspenders under his suit coat, and the woman carried a fan with Jesus' picture on the front. I looked up at the clock above the courthouse door. It said eight forty-eight. Another car pulled up, the fire chief's red-and-white Nova. He got out, a heavy man, and walked straight toward us like he knew who we were.

"Hell of a day to be cooped up in that jail, ain't it?" he said.

"Too hot to be anywhere," said Callahan, licking the cracks at the corners of his mouth.

"You come down to see the preacher?" Not getting a reply, the fire chief continued, "Biggest case that ever hit this town. You couldn't help but know he was a little crazy. Whiskey will do that to any man after a while. But, shoot, who would have thought he'd kill a girl like that?" The fire chief stuck a Camel in his mouth and slapped his pockets. "Got a light?"

Callahan shook his head.

"If you don't mind me saying so," the fire chief continued, taking the unlit cigarette from his mouth, "you both look a little crazy yourselves, sitting out here in the sun. Nobody else much come down for the arraignment. It'll be different when the jury selection starts. People live around here I haven't seen in fifteen years, but they'll be sitting in on this trial. Me, I'd like to watch the bastard hang. When I was seventeen I seen a hanging right here in front of this courthouse. They roped off the street." He sighted down his cigarette. "Biggest crowd I'd ever been in, except for a LSU ball game. Why, a widow lady got crushed against the gallows, so there was really two deaths that day. Me, I got as close as I could. I'd always been one for a little excitement. But damn if this friend of mine didn't ask me for a cigarette right when the nigger's feet came out from under him—he'd raped a white woman, this was 1936—so I didn't get to hear it."

"Hear what?" asked Callahan.

"Why, the sound of his neck breaking. What else?"

By the courthouse clock it was nine. Callahan and I got up to go in. I hadn't seen Sammy yet, but I guessed he was already inside.

The courtroom was paneled and air conditioned, like somebody's den. At first I didn't see the preacher, but then the two men leaning over his table moved away, arguing, and I caught a glimpse of the preacher's head. It shone like polished wood above his gray prisoner's shirt.

The old farm couple and the fire chief sat near the front, I suppose so they could hear every word. Callahan and I sat on the farthest back row near an air-conditioning vent. We hadn't bothered to disguise ourselves again. Now that Rain was dead, what difference did it make? In a way, I hoped Sammy wouldn't show up. I wouldn't if I'd been him. Maybe he'd gone to Detroit to stay with his aunt. Or maybe he'd just taken off with no clear idea of where he was going, except that he was getting away from here.

The judge came in wearing a regular suit and wire-rimmed glasses that reflected the overhead lights. A woman I hadn't noticed before was sitting at a little table off to the side, looking through a folder as she pulled her hair behind her ears. The deputy with cauliflower ears, who had walked in right behind the judge, whispered something in the woman's ear, and laughed. She didn't seem to think anything was funny and gave him a look to let him know. "Your Honor," she said, "since defendant and counsel are present, may we begin?"

"This arraignment is set for nine o'clock," the judge said, "and according to my watch, we're already running a little late. Bailiff?"

The deputy with cauliflower ears mumbled a few words in front of the American flag. "Very well," the judge continued, but he stopped when the door in back opened. I turned to look. In walked a tall black woman with frosted hair and a plain black dress tied with a sash. She carried herself like everybody there was supposed to know exactly who she was. I figured it must have been Sammy's aunt Eunice, because right behind her came Sammy in a suit and white shirt with a short black tie askew beneath his face. He didn't see me as they moved down the aisle to a bench nearer the front, and I kept myself from calling out to him as he stood aside to let his aunt into her seat.

The judge looked thoughtfully at them a moment and then swiveled his chair to face the preacher's table. "Which one of you gentlemen is the defendant, Reverend Ephraim Jackson Smith?"

The two men in suits at the preacher's table laughed, but the judge just lifted an eyebrow at them and they hushed. The preacher, meanwhile, had raised his hand.

"Thank you, Reverend Smith," said the judge. "Would you be kind enough to approach the bench?"

One of the men in suits showed the preacher where to stand, and for the first time I noticed a short man in shirtsleeves clacking away at a little machine.

"Now, I'm sure you're aware," the judge said, "of the general nature of the charges against you. However, this is a formal proceeding during which our district attorney, Miss Birkwith, will read those charges to you exactly as they appear on the indictment, and then I will ask you to tell me, with the help and advice of your counsel, how you plead."

The preacher nodded, but I couldn't listen to any more. The place was too much like a funeral parlor. I had to get air, some water to drink.

Without saying a word to Callahan I slid out of the bench and pushed through the swinging doors. The slap of my tennis shoes echoed down the hall. At the end stood a marble water fountain. It was bathed in a pool of light from a window near the ceiling. The word COLORED had been painted over a long time ago, but I could still see the outline of the letters above the marble. I twisted the faucet, staring with one eye and then the other at my reflection in the metal drain. Then I took the longest drink of water I'd ever had. I drank until I couldn't even swallow the last mouthful. Instead, I threw back my head, blinking at the light from the window, and let the water run out the corners of my mouth and down the sides of my neck. That must have been when it happened. I felt someone in line behind me, and I slowly turned around.

It was Rain.

"Lizard?" she said. "How did you know where to find me?"

The hair on my arms was rising. I tried, but couldn't speak.

"You're shaking," she said. "Are you cold?"

"The pump house was empty," I finally said.

"I had to leave the pump house," she said.

"And the orchard."

"The orchard too. Are you all right? You look like you don't feel well."

"I'm scared," I said.

"What of? Is somebody after you?"

"You're dead."

Rain shook her head, confused, then her face gave way in relief. "Oh, I see what you thought. You've got it all wrong. It's Mama who's dead. We thought she had drowned. But Sammy found her bones in the cave." She shuddered under her thin white dress. "She was murdered," she said, and looked down. "The preacher killed her and buried her in the cave two years ago this past spring."

My fingers were still tingling, but I was no longer afraid.

"Are you all right?" she said.

I nodded. "Are you?"

"Sure, Lizard. I'm fine. So's Sammy. We're living with Aunt Eunice. She left Detroit the minute she found out the preacher had been arrested." She leaned forward to take a drink of water. Her braids had been pulled up in back, coiled, and pinned with a turquoise barrette.

She wiped her mouth on the back of her hand. "How was Birmingham?" she asked.

I told her about the play while we walked slowly down the hall toward the courtroom. Just then the doors swung open, and Callahan came out smiling. "I know," he said when I started to speak. "I talked to Sammy." Then he stopped short, running his hand over his whiskered face. "You must be Rain. I'm Callahan, a friend of Lizard's."

"You're an actor," Rain said.

"More or less. I'm sorry about your mother."

"Thank you," Rain said. "Mama would appreciate that."

"Rain, you missed everything!" Sammy yelled as he bulled out of the courtroom in front of his aunt Eunice.

"Why would I want to see the preacher again, anyway?" Rain answered, her hands on her hips.

"But he tried to escape. The deputy had to handcuff him and drag him away!"

Rain lowered her voice. "We're in a public place, Sammy. Remember what Mama would say."

Sammy turned on his aunt in a fury. "That's what I've been telling you about. That's all I hear out of her. Mama this and Mama that. You'd think Mama wasn't in her grave. You'd think she was prowling around spying on us. You got to make Rain stop doing that. I'm turning thirteen next May. You hear me, thirteen!"

Sammy's aunt leaned close to him. "And that's too old to be sassing your older sister or screaming at your aunt Eunice."

Sammy stood struck by his aunt's words. "So that's the way it's going to be, huh? The flower of my manhood trampled by two old black hens!"

"Sammy?" Aunt Eunice growled. "Didn't I hear your older sister telling you to lower your voice among polite company?"

"Polite company? You call this crippled-up white trash polite?" he said, wrinkling his nose at me. "And this other one look like he slept the night on the floor of a cattle car, and you're talking to me about 'polite'?"

"Now, that's enough out of you, Samuel! We'll see if your behind knows the meaning of 'polite'!"

"You wouldn't dare touch me. Come on, Lizard."

Sammy grabbed my hand and started pulling me down the hallway, through the glass doors, and out into the white, even heat. He didn't stop until we were down the steps and into the parking lot, under a tree. There he turned to me, suddenly calm and sure, as if he had a secret and all this hollering at his family had been an excuse so he could get away and tell me.

"Behind Auntie's house," he said, "there's a creek." He waited to let that sink in. "We'll gig crawdads there this afternoon. All right?"

16

THE SHOWER came up so suddenly that the wind took down the sign in front of Thompson's Seed and Feed. Callahan and I ran for the truck. When I slammed the door shut, he was grinning. "Their aunt's some woman," he said. We stopped at the boardinghouse long enough for him to run in and pay for the night before. He left the engine running, and I watched the rain spatter on the hood and steam away. Then, almost as quickly as it had started, the rain gusted and stopped. Behind me the main street of my hometown gleamed.

All the way to Newllano, Callahan played the radio loud. The windows were down, and the air smelled clean. It had been a real storm up this way. Some pines were down in a field, and an empty horse trailer had flipped on its side.

At the only traffic light in Newllano, Callahan turned left. Rain's aunt Eunice had told him where to go. The house she rented was the second on the right after the intersection, with oaks in the front yard and a dogtrot through the center. Once the house had been white. Now it needed paint, and the brickwork underneath the porch was falling away. But because of the sudden rain the tarpaper roof glistened like new, and the bantam roosters from the house next door, pecking for grubs in Aunt Eunice's front yard, gave the place a lived-in, permanent look.

Callahan cut the engine and said, "I knew Rain was alive all along."

He thought a lot of himself, I decided, but I liked him anyway.

Sammy met us at the door. "This ain't so great," he said, "but I can put up with it for a couple of years, until I go off to West Point, that is. This here is the sitting room, where my sister, Rain, will entertain her beaus. And that does not include some people I know." He glared at me. I didn't see any furniture in the house except for an overstuffed recliner and some folding aluminum chairs. But in the kitchen was an icebox and stove. Rain and her aunt Eunice were already at work slicing okra and onions and shiny green peppers for the gumbo they were making. The batter for corn fritters stood ready on a cabinet top.

"Come on," Sammy said. "I'll show you what I was talking about."

"Wait a minute. I'm coming too," Rain said.

But Sammy was already out the door, with me right behind. The backyard sloped through hackberry bushes and wild honeysuckle to a line of trees that bordered the creek. The water was blood-red from the morning rain, quick and swirling in the narrow spots, but spreading thick and syrupy where the banks were low. Sammy had a white pine stick with a nail driven in the end. He leaned on it as he peered into the creek.

"Can't see a damn thing," he said. "We'll have to wait till the mud settles, and that might take all day." But when he investigated the pools where the bank was eroded and the current hadn't disturbed the bottom, he had better luck. Quickly he gigged two crawfish and flipped them onto the bank. They arched their bony backs and stretched their claws, opening and closing their pinchers in pain, while the nail holes oozed green liquid and their antennas swiveled as if to find out what had injured them so bad.

Rain came on us breathless, holding a long pole with a net at the end. "Don't gig them, Sammy. You'll spoil the meat. The gumbo'll be ruined."

"What do you know about it, Rain? You're afraid to touch them anyway."

"We'll see about that," she answered, handing the pole with the net to me.

While I jumped the creek at a narrow spot, Sammy and Rain competed for the same pool. Sammy poked under the rocks Rain lifted, even before she had a chance to see what was underneath. Suddenly Rain reached in up to her elbow and came out holding the biggest crawfish I'd ever seen. Its heavy pinchers waved helplessly in the air. "How do you like that!" she shouted, and I waved back at her with the net.

In not much time we had a dozen apiece, although Rain said her aunt couldn't use Sammy's. "I didn't want to eat them, anyway," he said. "I'm going to put them in the icebox and use them for bait."

But before we walked back up to the house, Sammy had another idea. "You think it's deep enough to swim?"

It didn't take us long to find out. We waded till the creek dropped to form a larger pool. Old lumber had dammed it up. Then we took off our clothes and went in up to our waists. Because of the rain the water on top was cold. The old lumber creaked like a flatboat as our waves washed against it.

"Look at me," Sammy cried. "I'm a duck." And he made his hands like duckbills and drank from the creek like a duck.

"I'm an otter!" Rain said. She disappeared head first without a sound. So I pretended to be an alligator, with my arms in front like huge jaws and my legs going from side to side like a tail.

When I came up for air, Rain and Sammy were frozen side by side, looking up. On the end of an overhead branch rested a butterfly as big as one of Rain's hands. It was yellow and black, with eyespots that were the deepest red, and it moved its wings so gently while it balanced on the branch that it seemed to be breathing the sunlight that fell to the water below.

Without a word Rain waded behind her brother and, still looking up, put her hands on his shoulders. He knew without asking to duck underwater, and she climbed onto his shoulders before he slowly rose up, water streaming down his sides. It was clear to me now that she wanted the butterfly to light on her outstretched hand. She and Sammy strained together toward the branch, so close that the pattern of the butterfly's wings moved slowly across Rain's face. And at the point when it looked like Sammy and Rain had escaped gravity and turned into something miraculous themselves, their aunt Eunice shouted: "Rain!" They wavered a moment, then fell, Rain tumbling forward into the creek, and when they

came up sputtering, the butterfly was gone, bobbing and
weaving upstream between the trees.

Aunt Eunice's voice was soft, but firm. "I'm ashamed
of you, Rain. And on the very day after your mama's
funeral! Now, put back on your clothes and follow me to
the house."

Rain's head was bowed as she waded out of the creek.
She didn't look at us or say good-bye, but got dressed on
the bank behind a live oak tree and then, carrying her
shoes, followed her aunt through the honeysuckle toward the house.

We ate corn fritters, gumbo with whole red peppers,
tomatoes, sweet Vidalia onions, and iced tea. Rain and I
sat on the lowest front step, Sammy above us at the top.
Callahan and Aunt Eunice were in folding chairs on the
porch, Callahan's legs crossed at the knee, his heaped-up
plate in his lap. He and Aunt Eunice talked all through
the meal, their voices low and musical in the gathering
dusk.

Aunt Eunice was remembering her life before, when
she and her sister, Ruth, Rain's mother, used to walk into
Newllano for flour, sugar, and rice. "There was a feeling
then," she said, "that we all belonged to the same land.
When I moved to Detroit, I couldn't tell my sister good-
bye. I was ashamed. I felt it was my duty to stay, but that
old northern city just kept calling me. It told me I wanted
to live free, paint my nails, have a walk-up apartment
where nobody knew my name. And I got what I wanted,
more than I wanted. Got married to another anonymous
person, an artist, a musician and poet. A rare find. We led
a life, children, but don't bring this up again. We led a
sweet, sad life where you'd make a friend one night and

by morning have forgotten his name. Laughing in powder rooms, smoking thin cigarettes, listening to jazz. These are the times, I kept thinking to myself. I hope I never forget these times."

Callahan stopped chewing and looked up. The cicadas had started.

"Then your mother died, Rain. And my artist got busted for dealing drugs. His poetry wasn't so hot anyway. I wanted so bad to come back and take care of you two, but there wasn't any money. We'd been living on air. So I got a job at night in a hospital, and I tried to save, but the rent kept going up, along with the gas, electricity, and eggs. That walk-up apartment wasn't so romantic anymore. The stairs had begun to hurt my legs."

"Tell us how you got the money to come here," Sammy said.

"Who said I've got money?"

"For the train ticket and the first month's rent," Sammy insisted, "and those clothes you bought me for school."

Aunt Eunice laughed her low, manly, musical laugh. "Honey, I discovered there are always ways to get back where you belong if you want to bad enough." Rain smiled up at her, and Callahan stretched out his legs.

"And anyway, if things get any worse, I can always find something around here to sell."

Sammy and Rain looked expectantly at me. At first I didn't know why, but then I remembered the silver bowl that wasn't silver. I knew I'd have to tell them now. "I'll be back in a minute," I said, and I slowly got up.

The bowl lay on the seat of the truck. I cradled it under my arm and walked back to the porch. The fireflies were winking all around us, green and gold. In my sadness they seemed like they were looking for something that was lost, and their lights, which had been so strong, were fading now, and going out one by one.

"I couldn't sell it," I said when I reached their round faces on the steps and on the porch. "The museum director said it was only worth fifty dollars at the most."

Aunt Eunice suddenly broke out in a smile. "Lord, child, where did you find this?" She leaned toward me, took the bowl, and turned it slowly in her hands. "I can't believe this old thing is still around. Children, this bowl almost came between your mother and me. I thought she'd thrown it away years ago!"

"Thrown it away?" Sammy said. "Mama wasn't that crazy, was she, Rain?"

Rain acted like she hadn't heard.

"Was she?" Sammy repeated.

"What *was* that boy's name?" Aunt Eunice said. When she looked up, each of her eyes reflected a sliver of new moon. "It was a fine-sounding name like Caesar or Hannibal."

Callahan winked at me. I'd almost forgotten he was there, his feet stretched out before him and one of his shirt collars standing straight up.

"Napoleon!" Aunt Eunice finally said. "That name alone was enough to attract me to him. Napoleon, the saltwater-taffy man."

"What's that got to do with the silver bowl?" Sammy asked.

"Let Aunt Eunice tell her story," Rain said.

"Callahan, you remember saltwater taffy, don't you?" Aunt Eunice hugged the bowl to her wide, muscular chest.

"Yes'm," he answered.

"It's a candy, Sammy, that sticks to your teeth. It's hard to chew but just as sweet as can be. Now, you can find taffy in some five-and-dimes, wrapped up in boxes with big price tags. But it gets hard as rocks in those boxes. It loses its specialness. There used to be only one place to get taffy fresh and warm—in October at the Beauregard Parish Fair. They had a machine in the Conservation tent that made saltwater taffy by pulling it like this." She set the bowl in her lap and did her arms like paddle wheels pulling against one another while they turned. "If you got it right when it came out of the machine, chopped into pieces and wrapped in wax paper, it'd be hot enough to warm your pockets. And the taste! Well, you've simply got to try some to know what I mean."

"I'll do that," Sammy said. "Now, what about the bowl?"

"I'm getting to the bowl," Aunt Eunice said with some heat in her voice. "As I said, Napoleon operated that machine. I never knew his last name. Your mother didn't, either, as far as I know. She wouldn't mention him at all after this particular October fair week. It was the year your grandmother went to bed with a broken ankle. That lousy doctor in Leesville didn't set it straight. So one of us sisters had to stay at the house all the time. Ruth and I couldn't go to the fair together, you see. We had to alternate nights, if we were going at all. Which was fine with me."

"Why?" Sammy asked.

"Because I had an interest in Napoleon, the saltwater taffy man, and I didn't like the idea of my younger sister tagging along after me when I went to see him."

"I bet I know what happened," Rain said. "Mama was seeing him, too, on the nights when you weren't."

Aunt Eunice nodded emphatically. "You're smarter than I was, Rain. Now, why couldn't I see that back then, instead of making myself sick on saltwater taffy and spending every bit of my harvest money? Ruth didn't say a thing to let on what she was doing. And neither did that lying Napoleon. He told me—well, he told me a lot of things. But not one word from my sister."

"But you didn't tell Mama, either, did you?" Sammy asked.

"No, I didn't tell Ruth, for the same reason no girl tells. I wanted him all for myself. Just let somebody know where your affections lie, and first thing you know that somebody is trying to have the very same man." She paused to get her composure back. "But this is what happened on that October night, although you'd never have known it was October. It was more like July, a hot, heavy night. Didn't even seem like fair time. In the afternoon the clouds had been low and gray. I was afraid my night at the fair would be rained out, and this was the very last night. But the sky held back. I hitched a ride to the fairgrounds when I finished helping the widow next door bring in her cows. The Conservation tent was crowded, but I pushed through the folks around the saltwater-taffy machine and smiled into the eyes of that rascal Napoleon. I don't know what it was about him. He wasn't the type I'd gone with until then. He had a thin face and a sweet way. I guess he's the reason I hung out with poets when I moved up North. Maybe he was a poet himself. I don't know. He lied like one."

"Mama was there, wasn't she?" Rain said.

"Goodness, Rain, can you read minds? Of course my

sister Ruth was there, standing in line with the rest of them, waiting on that hot saltwater taffy, with some story about your grandmother feeling sorry for her since this was the fair's last night. I knew she'd probably cried and got your grandmother's sympathy. Forgive me for saying so, but she probably did. So when Napoleon took his thirty-minute break, he had two girls who wanted to share his time—me and my younger sister, Ruth. I made sure he knew she was only sixteen. But that just seemed to make him more interested. Oh, it wasn't a pretty scene, children. My knuckles were hard as gravel as we walked together down the midway, me on one side of him and Ruth on the other. I think he was afraid to take either one of our hands. He played a few of the games along the way but didn't seem to have any luck."

"I bet the trouble really started when he won a prize," Rain said.

"I should say so." Aunt Eunice scowled. "It was the coin toss. I think Napoleon was trying not to win so he wouldn't have to make his choice, or maybe he didn't think that far ahead. Anyway, he flipped a dime out and rung a beautiful silver-looking bowl, this one right here, with flowers and fruit adorning its edge. I thought it was the finest bowl I'd ever seen. Maybe I said so. Maybe that's the reason he smiled and handed it to me. I was touched, but the gesture was too much for Ruth. She read more into the gift than he had intended, I think. Off she ran down the midway. 'Ruth!' he hollered after her. 'I'll win you one too!' But it was plain too late. Your mama was fast."

"And the storm was picking up," Rain said.

Aunt Eunice just looked at her this time. "Did your mother tell you this story?"

"No," Rain said. She shook her head like she'd been dreaming. "It's just that you mentioned the clouds, and the sky holding back."

"Not for much longer, though," Aunt Eunice said. "We could already hear thunder. The wind was whipping at the tent flaps. Some of the concession people hurried to take in their stuffed animals so they wouldn't get wet. I said to Napoleon, 'Let's find a dry place to ride out the rain.' But he said he was worried about my sister, so we kept walking up the midway. I hugged that bowl. I'd never owned a thing so beautiful. 'Who cares what happens to Ruth?' I said, but I knew by the way Napoleon looked at me that it was a mean thing to say. I particularly regretted it when lightning struck awful close, and all the lights on the midway went out. People started milling about, and soon we overheard someone say the Ferris wheel had stuck. 'There's somebody stuck at the top,' they added while the lightning flashed all around us. Both me and Napoleon must have had the same thought, because we ran to the Ferris wheel and discovered the girl at the top was Ruth. I hollered up to her, 'Everything'll be all right, sister!' But she just shouted back, 'I hope I never come down.' She said something else, but the words were lost in the rolling thunder. When the lightning flashed, you could see her thin arms against the red-and-yellow gondola. It swayed in the wind. And then the bottom of the sky fell out. I'd never seen such rain. It was a solid wall."

"How did he get to her?" Rain asked.

"Who?"

"Napoleon."

"Now, how did you know he climbed that Ferris wheel?"

"That's what I was asking you," Rain said.

"Oh." Aunt Eunice looked at her suspiciously and then continued. "That crazy saltwater-taffy man stole a tarp from over a hot-tamale cart, threw it over his shoulder, and took out in the rain. I screamed at him to stop before he got electrocuted, but he couldn't have heard me, and even if he had, it didn't slow him down one bit. I'd never seen a man take such a chance. He proceeded to climb up the steel framework of that Ferris wheel while the lightning danced all around. Now and then the great wheel turned a foot, and everybody on the ground gasped as he held on with both hands. We lost sight of him near the top behind a gust of rain, but it lifted a second long enough for me to see him at the end as he swung into the gondola and pulled that tarp over his and your mother's heads."

"Weren't you jealous?" Rain asked.

"Heavens no, honey. Not then. I was relieved and proud. And gradually the lightning moved out over the fields and into the next parish. The rain kept up heavy for a while, though. I stood under the awning of the Conservation tent, clutching my silver bowl and watching for Napoleon's head. At last the storm stopped lashing the tent flaps. It settled into a light, warm rain, almost like spring instead of October, a tender drizzle, but still he and your mother hadn't come out from under that tarp. The gondola swayed. I wondered what they were doing up there. And something changed inside of me while I waited. So that when the rain completely stopped, and they got the Ferris wheel running again, and Napoleon and your mother threw the tarp back and stepped out onto the ground, the first thing I did was hand her that silver bowl. I wouldn't need it where I was going. For I'd made up my mind to head North, find my own life, and leave the rest of this behind."

"And I wasn't born yet, was I?" Rain asked.

Aunt Eunice looked at her a minute. "Why, no, child, you came along after that."

"Not bad," Sammy said. "The part about the lightning especially. But I've got a better story about the bowl. I've got the best. When Chief Narrow Meadow's niece was kidnapped—"

Suddenly Callahan woke himself with a loud snort. "It can't be two o'clock," he said.

"Who said anything about two o'clock?" Sammy said.

"What?" Callahan blinked. "I'm sorry. I must have fallen asleep."

"I'll tell you what you need," said Aunt Eunice. "We got quilts enough for all of us. You and Lizard make pallets on the floor."

"Oh, no," Callahan said. "I couldn't do that."

"I bet you could."

Aunt Eunice was right. The quilts were deep and warm, and Callahan was snoring before the smile had disappeared from his face.

I slept too. And that night I dreamed somebody had locked me up in the quiet room at the Leesville State School. I didn't know what I'd done to get there. I only knew the tile was cold. The shadow of the bars fell across my arm. But in the distance I heard the jingling of keys. My friend Mike appeared, his right arm waggling, and with a laugh he set me free. Then he woke Walrus and Ricardo and all the rest of the boys. Together we streamed out into the night, hollering and slapping each other on the back. Everyone got away, even the boy without any hands. And the last thing I saw in my dream was a table full of albinos in the Dari-Delite across the highway. They were sharing a huge milkshake with straws enough to go around while they watched the lighted trucks on the highway speed by.

I woke up with a tingling in my head. It was the first good sleep I'd had in a long time. I tiptoed into Rain's room and shook her lightly until she opened her eyes.

"I've got to go now. Tell Callahan I'll be okay."

"But you've got to stay for breakfast. We'll have honey and biscuits," she said.

I shook my head, sure that Aunt Eunice would want me to live in Newllano or that Callahan would drag me to Houston with him. They wouldn't understand what I needed to do. But Rain, without knowing, did.

I gave her the wooden crescent Willie Tyson had made and told her to remember me by it. We agreed that if I was in these parts, we'd see each other again in October at the Beauregard Parish Fair.

When I got to the highway, I looked back once and tried to memorize Aunt Eunice's house among the trees at dawn, with the porch light still burning and Callahan's truck parked in the yard, a bantam rooster pecking at the gravel by the right front tire.

Ahead of me the highway was a long black snake, disappearing in mist where it crossed the creek. I knelt long enough to tighten my shoelaces.

"Lizard!"

I knew it was Callahan, and when I looked up I could just make out his silhouette behind the screen door of Aunt Eunice's house. He stepped barefoot onto the porch, down the steps, and across the damp grass toward me. "What are you doing?" he asked. He glanced up the highway. "Where do you think you're going?"

"I'm going to find my daddy," I said.

"I thought your father was dead."

I could have slugged him. "You're the one who told me he was alive."

"Now, listen to me."

"On the roof of that hotel in Birmingham," I said.

"I thought we'd been through all that," he said. "I was drunk. I meant it metaphorically."

"What the hell does that mean?"

"It means I was being a stupid, mean son of a bitch. I didn't know what I was talking about. I don't know who your father is, or whether he's dead or alive. I didn't even remember that night on the roof until you told me about it. I was in a blackout, Lizard, don't you understand?"

"Well, I'm going anyway," I said. "If he's alive, I'll find him." I turned and started down the shoulder of the highway toward the creek and its row of dark pines.

"Wait up," Callahan said, but I kept walking. I heard him picking his way over the gravel behind me and knew he was going to take me by the shoulder before he actually did.

"Look," he said, "I just can't let you take off by yourself like this," he said. "When you're older it'll be different."

"You didn't care about how old I was when you let me go to Birmingham with you."

"I can't undo what's been done," he said. "But now I don't have any choice. I've got to see to it that you get back home."

"I'm not going back to the state school," I said.

He dropped his hands. "I didn't say the state school," he said. "I said home."

I looked at him with first one eye and then the other.

Callahan sighed. Then he shoved his hands into the pockets of his jeans and glanced out over the fields toward the row of pines that were just now beginning to stand out clear against the morning sky.

"I guess we're going to have to find Miss Cooley," he said.

17

BROUSSARD is a common name in Alexandria, Louisiana. Alton Broussard is not. So we didn't have any trouble finding his number and rural route in the phone book. But nobody answered the phone, and when we drove out to his place off the highway near Valentine Lake, we were greeted by two unfriendly dogs that looked like they had German shepherd in them. There weren't any cars parked in the carport of Broussard's brick farmhouse with a TV antenna on top (I couldn't help but be pleased that Miss Cooley had come up so in the world), and neither he nor Miss Cooley came to the door when Callahan knocked.

By then it was almost noon, and Callahan thought we should go back into Alexandria to eat. He found a café near the Rapides Parish courthouse. The food, he said, would most likely be good and cheap, as it had to satisfy the courthouse-lawyer crowd—it's a sure thing he had never eaten at the L&N—and we'd probably find out

anything we needed to know there. With this in mind he
struck up a conversation with the first old man who sat
down next to him at the counter, a retired grocer who
recently had had a stroke. The stroke had affected his
memory in peculiar ways, he said. He could not remember the names of his two oldest children or what he had
eaten that morning for breakfast, but he knew all about
the many varieties of Broussards in Alexandria, even the
name of the oil drilling equipment company that Alton
Broussard worked for.

"He used to come into the store," the grocer said. "He
was a snotty little kid."

Callahan called the equipment company while the
waitress went to get our ice cream and peach cobbler,
but they said Mr. Alton Broussard was out with a client,
so we took our time with dessert. When Callahan called
back later, they told him Broussard had come back in but
then checked out for the day, so we rode back to Broussard's house off the highway out near Valentine Lake. A
huge storm front had spilled in from Texas and it chose
to let loose just as we pulled back into Broussard's gravel
drive. This time a red Malibu was parked under the carport.

"Wait here," Callahan said. "I'll be right back." He put
an arm above his head to shield himself from the rain and
used the other arm to fend off Broussard's dogs, who
were not so much fierce, it seemed, as starved for affec-
tion and afraid of storms.

Callahan knocked loudly at the door, a light came on in
the living room and on the front porch, and someone let
him in. He couldn't have been inside the house more
than fifteen minutes, during which time I watched light-

ning strike a dozen times, real close, through the trees in the direction of Valentine Lake.

When Callahan reemerged from the house and bolted for the car, he was nursing his right hand.

"She's not here," he said. His hair was plastered to his forehead with rainwater. "They didn't get married after all. According to Broussard, Miss Cooley moved back to De Ridder without giving him back his ring."

"What happened to your hand?" I asked.

"Broussard is an ornery little son of a bitch," he said. "You're going to have to help me shift gears."

So the trip back to De Ridder was much longer than the trip up, what with me grinding the gears and the rain so heavy at times that even with the wipers going full speed, Callahan swore he couldn't see.

"I mean, what really happened about your hand?" I said when we had passed the last of the Kisatchie National Forest. "Did you hit him?"

"I tried to," Callahan said, "but the door to the broom closet got in the way."

"Why?"

"It was just there is all."

"I mean, why'd you try to hit him?"

"He was curious about why I wanted to find Miss Cooley and when I tried to explain, he said some things that teed me off."

"Like?"

"Nothing worth repeating," he said.

But I knew it must have been about me.

The storm dispersed just as we hit that stretch of four-lane before the De Ridder city limits sign. It had been a big storm but fast moving, and by the time Callahan pulled the truck to the curb in front of the L&N Café, it was hard to believe there had been such a downpour in the first place. I rolled my window down, and the air was soft and a bit cooler now that the storm had passed. The frogs were starting to come out, but they weren't so loud you couldn't hear the ticking of the cooling truck engine or the distant sound of the black kids skating in the parking lot of Thompson's Seed and Feed. It was a quarter to eight by the clock in the courthouse tower. This being Wednesday, the L&N would stay open till ten to catch the late shift from the turpentine plant.

Mr. Smithers had just closed up his barber shop across Pine Street from the L&N. He stayed late, too, on Wednesday nights. I didn't wave at him because I think he had always been a little scared of me.

"Well," Callahan said, "what are we waiting for?"

"I'm not going in," I said.

"Why not?"

"I just don't want to right now."

"You don't even know she's here."

"She's here," I said. The plate glass windows in front were still fogged a little from the storm, but I could see Miss Cooley's back in an unfogged space between the N and the word CAFÉ. She was wearing the pink T-shirt with a tiger on back that the sergeant from Fort Polk had brought her from Thailand. It was just a glimpse, but enough to be sure.

"What does she look like?" Callahan asked.

I pictured her in my head. "She's skinny and wearing a tiger shirt. And she's got blue eyes. She's probably the only one working tonight."

"You sure you don't want to come on in with me?" he asked.

I shook my head.

"Maybe she'll come out," he said.

I shrugged.

"Well, just stay put," he said. "And don't turn on the radio. You'll run the battery down."

He got out of the truck and hitched up his jeans, patting his pocket to make sure he had his keys and pocket comb. At first I thought he'd dropped something, but he was only bent down to check the front tires. I think he was just scared, but he was a good enough actor to straighten himself up before he went inside.

No sooner had he walked in the door of the café than I got the urge to take a walk around the block. The black kids stopped skating long enough to stare after my limp, but one of them recognized me and told the rest of them to pay attention to their game. I walked past the old elementary school where I'd sometimes wished I could have gone. It didn't look like such hot stuff now that I'd seen a little of the world.

Market Street was empty. The swallows that nested under the eaves of the old railroad station whirled above the tracks. In the distance I could see the stacks of the turpentine plant. Behind them the sun had set in a bank of yellow and purple clouds. I didn't feel too good about myself right then. I'd come too far to balk at facing Miss Cooley. But the reason I hadn't gone into the café was simple. I was just afraid she wouldn't want me back.

Returning down the alley that connected with Pine, I heard the café's screen door bang shut. Callahan had probably come out to get me, seen I wasn't in the truck, and gone back inside.

I was curious now about what might be going on between them, so I climbed into the sweet gum tree by the garbage cans and shinnied out on the branch nearest the

L&N's side door. Above the door was an exhaust fan, and I'd learned long ago that when the fan wasn't running, I could hear the conversation going on inside. When the fan started up—it was run by thermostat—I'd get a blast of hot air and couldn't hear a thing. This time I had to wait till the fan stopped before I could get close enough to hear.

At first I wasn't sure it was Callahan talking, but then he coughed in midsentence and a chair scraped, and I knew it was him, still nervous about facing Miss Cooley, I guess.

"Now, that's one thing that I don't think is any of your business, do you?" she said.

"No, ma'am, I don't guess it is," he said. "Just curious is all."

"Well, it's nothing that matters anyway now. The truth is, I don't know who his father was."

"What do you mean?"

"I mean, I was seeing two men at the time. The one I was in love with was married. The other one was his friend."

"What happened to them?" Callahan asked.

"The friend got killed in a fight on the oil rigs, don't ask me over what. The man I loved wouldn't leave his wife. I'll never forgive him for that. Sometimes I wish that he was the one that had died."

"So what happened when Lucius came along?"

"My family—I got a drunk for a daddy and two crazed half-sisters—they'd already disowned me for running around with a married man. I moved up here the minute I started to show. I was only fifteen, but I knew a trucker who had a load of stumps for the turpentine plant. Nobody in this place cared who I was. I could start out fresh. I'd had it with Lafayette anyway."

"Will you ever move back?"

"Why?"

"Doesn't the place where you were born call you?"

"That's just a bunch of talk. There's nothing for me down there."

"Why didn't you tell Lucius you were his mother?" Callahan said.

"Are you a social worker?"

"No, ma'am."

"Okay, listen, if he was retarded bad as everybody said, the less he knew the better, right? What difference would it make? If he wasn't retarded, he'd figure it out soon enough. Can we talk about something else?"

"Who said he was retarded?"

"What else would you think about somebody who stares at insects all day and don't want to get out with the other boys and play ball and such as that? And I'm not even talking about the way he looks."

"Do you love him?"

There was a silence, during which I imagine Miss Cooley leaned over to pour Callahan another cup of coffee. "You don't know much about love, do you?" she said.

"No, ma'am, I don't guess I do."

"That's right, because if you did, you wouldn't have to ask a question like that."

The exhaust fan kicked on. I waited, but I couldn't hear a thing. When it stopped, nobody was talking. I heard the screen door out front bang shut and the truck engine cranking up. Miss Cooley rounded the corner about then. She had one hand on her hip.

"Lucius!" she yelled. Then she saw me in the tree, and she stopped. Her chipped tooth glistened in the twilight.

"I should have known you'd be up there," she said. "I guess you heard what we've been talking about."

I didn't say anything.

"We'll discuss it later on. But right now, why don't you come inside and get something to eat."

I still didn't say anything.

"Lucius, I am talking to you, son."

"My name is Lizard now," I said.

"Is it?" she said. "Well, things do change. Still, you ought to come in."

"It's too early yet."

"Suit yourself," she said. "Just don't let the mosquitoes eat you up out here."

I watched her walk back around the corner, her bath slippers slapping against her feet. For the first time I realized that Miss Cooley was not that much older than I was, and like me she had a lot still to learn. It is true that I had missed her in my travels, but I knew then how things between us would have to turn out. I'd stay with her for a little while longer, at least till I turned sixteen. After that I'd be keeping my options open. In ways, I was already on my own.

That was the last day of July and already it's October, almost fair time. I'm in the sixth grade at the De Ridder Elementary School. It's an experiment, Miss Cooley says, but my teacher thinks that maybe after Christmas I can skip to the junior high and be with kids my own age. The sixth graders are scared of me. I'm not any bigger than they are, but I look a lot different, my voice has changed, and I'm also more experienced. For one thing, I've been to Birmingham and acted in a Shakespeare play. When the class was discussing where we should go on our fall field trip, I suggested the Leesville State School for Retarded Boys. The turpentine plant won out. I'm learning more about the two men who could have been my father. The one who worked on the rigs also played in a Cajun band—not the accordion, Miss Cooley says, but the steel guitar. He was missing the ring finger on his left hand. The married one moved with his family to someplace out West, where his kids are probably grown now. "Good riddance," Miss Cooley says. But talking about the men in her life gives us something to do at night, when we aren't watching the TV she bought with my first aid-to-dependent-children check. Callahan saw to it that she applied on my behalf. He and Sallie have split up for good now, but I guess that is for the best. He wrote a letter from Houston to tell me that and to let me know that Mr. Howell had passed away, something I think I knew was about to happen, and that Willie Tyson had moved to New York City, to a place called the Lower East Side. Waldo is doing fine and wants me to try out for something called summer stock. I don't see how I can do that. Callahan also says in the letter that I should think kindly of him, that he never meant any harm, and that he is counting on seeing Miss Cooley and me and Rain and her family when he comes back to De Ridder for the Beauregard Parish Fair.

I didn't know any of this on that night at the end of July, when I sat in the branches of the sweet gum tree and watched Callahan's truck pull away from the curb. All I knew was that I hated to see him go. It's true he was not my real father, but he might as well have been. I thought about jumping out of the tree and flagging him down to say good-bye, but I didn't. I just watched the truck turn the corner onto Highway 190, past the hospital and the funeral home and all the way to the fork in the road, where it bore to the left toward Lake Charles and Houston again.

I stayed in the tree until the streetlights came on and the insects struck up for the night. The sky was still blue in spite of that sliver of yellow moon in it. And I took some comfort in that fact. I'd forgotten how wide the sky was above the place where we lived, and how long during the summer it stayed light.

About the Author

DENNIS COVINGTON graduated from the University of Virginia and holds an MFA from the University of Iowa Writers' Workshop. He is now an associate professor of English at the University of Alabama at Birmingham, where he teaches fiction writing. His short stories have appeared in *Mississippi Review, Southern Exposure, The Greensboro Review,* and other magazines. *Lizard,* his first novel, is the winner of the Eighth Annual Delacorte Press Prize for a First Young Adult Novel. Dennis Covington is also a free-lance journalist whose articles on Central America have appeared in the Scripps-Howard and Newhouse newspapers and in *Vogue.* He lives just outside of his hometown of Birmingham with his wife, novelist Vicki Covington, and their two daughters.

YA F Cov⬛   IS 343783
Covington
Lizard   11/91